W

MW01074763

"Like a John Grisham novel, from the very start I was pulled right into the story and couldn't put the book down. It was as if I personally knew and cared about what happened to each of the main characters. Every chapter ended with so much excitement and suspense I had to continue to read until I learned how it ended, even though it kept me up until 3:00 A.M.

- Ray F., reader

DEAD IN THE WATER

"In Dead in the Water, R.J. Patterson accurately captures the action-packed saga of a what could be a real-life college football scandal. The sordid details will leave readers flipping through the pages as fast as a hurry-up offense."

- Mark Schlabach,
ESPN college sports columnist and
co-author of *Called to Coach*
and *Heisman: The Man Behind the Trophy*

THE WARREN OMISSIONS

"What can be more fascinating than a super high concept novel that reopens the conspiracy behind the JFK assassination while the threat of a global world war rests in the balance? With his new novel, *The Warren Omissions*, former journalist turned bestselling author R.J. Patterson proves he just might be the next worthy successor to Vince Flynn."

- Vincent Zandri
bestselling author of THE REMAINS

OTHER TITLES BY
R.J. PATTERSON

Cal Murphy Thrillers
Dead Shot
Dead Line
Better off Dead
Dead in the Water
Dead Man's Curve
Dead and Gone
Dead Wrong
Dead Man's Land
Dead Drop
Dead to Rights
Dead End

James Flynn Thrillers
The Warren Omissions
Imminent Threat
The Cooper Affair
Seeds of War

Brady Hawk Thrillers
First Strike
Deep Cover
Point of Impact
Full Blast
Target Zero
Fury
State of Play
Siege
Seek and Destroy
Into the Shadows
Hard Target
No Way Out
Two Minutes to Midnight
Against All Odds

AGAINST ALL ODDS

A Brady Hawk novel

R.J. PATTERSON

For Cal Powell, for great friendship
and seemingly infinite inside jokes

CHAPTER 1

Venice, Italy

HAWK ALWAYS IMAGINED snorkeling with his wife on his honeymoon, just not in the murky canal waters of Venice. This excursion wasn't part of the all-inclusive resort. Instead of coral reefs and colorful fish, his flashlight illuminated petrified wooden pilings and trash still making its way to the bottom of the water.

"You doing okay back there?" he asked, looking over his shoulder.

Alex flashed him a thumbs up.

Will she ever let me live this down? Going on a mission on our honeymoon? I'll never hear the end of it.

Hawk took a hard right and rolled over onto his back. The blue sky beaming down on them from above was still faintly visible. Seconds later, it vanished, covered by a gondola lazily moving along. However, there was still just enough light for Hawk to see an oar slice through the water near his head. He rolled away from the boat and waited until it eased down the canal and the overhead light returned.

"Almost there," he said.

Alex didn't say anything, and Hawk wasn't sure what that was a sign of. He suspected it wasn't good. When women go silent, he was preconditioned to believe he'd done something wrong. But Alex? She could be an enigma at times, instead caught up in contemplating something quietly. There was an equal chance that she was stewing over something he'd said during lunch or admiring the architectural brilliance of creating a city in the water out of nothing but wood.

Hawk checked his GPS coordinates and followed them to his left, leading right into the boat garage of Andrei Orlovsky, known Russian arms dealer. After surfacing for air, Hawk scanned his surroundings for a dock. He spotted it just on the other side of a sleek motorboat that contained far more horsepower than necessary on its outboard twin engines. As he swam around, he waited for Alex to appear. A few seconds later, her head bobbed out of the water with barely a splash. Operating stealthily was of utmost importance on this operation.

When Blunt called and requested Hawk and Alex go on a short mission, Hawk was hesitant. But Blunt made a strong case that they may not have a chance like this again. According to intelligence reports from the CIA, Orlovsky was in Venice on business for a few days and always took his laptop with him. The nearest operatives couldn't get to Venice and get outfitted before Orlovsky would be gone, disappearing again off the grid.

To his credit, Hawk asked Alex if she wanted to go. Her response was less than enthusiastic.

"How can we say no?" she said.

Hawk wasn't sure what she meant by that, but it signaled her willingness. He promptly conveyed the message to Blunt, who had equipment at their hotel room less than an hour later.

With Orlovsky scheduled to meet an African drug lord for lunch, Hawk and Alex seized the opportunity to go after the coveted intel: Orlovsky's contact list. The CIA had attempted to acquire the list in the past but failed when Orlovsky discovered the list had been stolen. He immediately enacted an emergency protocol with all his clients, alerting them of the theft. By the time the CIA attempted to utilize the information, it had been rendered useless. Phone numbers, addresses, emails—all changed or disabled and wiped away, with the exception of one. An arms buyer in Chechnya kept his information current and set an ambush for a covert CIA team, killing all of them. Such a brazen attack was the impetus behind the CIA aggressively pursuing the contact list yet again. The Chechnya buyer would be the first to pay.

Hawk eased out of the water and stripped out of his wetsuit. Alex opened her laptop, focused on her task.

"Being married makes these missions a little more fun," Hawk whispered.

She wagged her index finger at him and rolled her eyes.

Always such a stickler.

Hawk dressed in the clothes he'd brought with him in a bag. This time they had to make sure not a single trace of evidence, especially digital evidence, was left behind to signal that the list had been compromised.

Once Hawk finished dressing, he looked at Alex. She nodded and pointed at the door, signaling that she had rebooted the alarm system. A mainframe update would take down the security monitors for two minutes. She then hacked into the cameras and set up loops so Hawk could roam around the house without being seen.

He shoved the comlink in his ear and then eased inside.

"Do you have the flash drive?" she asked.

"Yep," Hawk whispered.

"Be careful. There are still two armed guards in

AGAINST ALL ODDS | 13

the house."

"Roger that."

Hawk crept upstairs and made his way into Orlovsky's study. The desktop was devoid of anything,
most notably a computer.

"There's nothing here," Hawk said.

"No computer?"

"Negative."

"Check the drawer."

Hawk gave it a tug, and it didn't budge. "It's
locked. How much time do I have?"

"Ninety seconds. Better hurry up and pick the
lock."

Hawk fiddled with the lock, and after a few seconds it gave way. He opened up drawer after drawer
and found nothing.

"Sixty seconds," Alex warned.

"There's no computer here."

"Can't be. Our intelligence report said he always
takes it with him."

Hawk knelt and rifled through a bunch of files.
"Wait a minute. I think I've found something. I found
a folder with a spreadsheet of a bunch of contacts.
This has to be it."

"Take a picture of it, and get out of there. You've
only got ten seconds before you'll be caught in dead
man's land."

Hawk whipped his phone out and snapped photo after photo of the eight-page document before shoving it back into the desk.

"You need to be leaving like twenty seconds ago," she said.

"I have to lock the drawer."

"Hawk! Get out of there now. You've got trouble headed your way."

"Grab my gear, and I'll meet you at the rendez-vous point."

"Are you crazy?"

"Just trust me."

Hawk grabbed a mail opener and jimmied the drawer locked. He had started an internal clock in his head and had about five seconds left before the cameras would restart and catch him in the room. But that was the least of his worries as he heard footsteps approaching down the hallway.

Hawk dashed across the room and climbed through the window that opened onto a small balcony extended over the water. He closed the door behind him and stood on the ledge. Wrapping his feet around the railing, he crouched to jump. The sound of the door latch clicking open in the study spurred him to take his leap.

He hit the dingy water with a loud splash. As he rolled over onto his back, he could see the opaque scene above—a man leaning out over the balcony glancing down at the water. After a few seconds, he closed the windows and returned inside.

But Hawk wasn't taking any chances. Harkening back to his Navy SEAL training, he held his breath and stayed beneath the surface as he swam. When he emerged, he was around the corner, staring directly at a gondola.

"I thought you were busted," Alex said, reaching her hand down to him.

Hawk gingerly climbed aboard, cautious not to rock the boat too much and tip them both.

"Did you get it?" she asked.

He smiled and held up his phone. "Gotta love innovative technology like waterproof phones."

"Great," Alex said. "Now let's get going."

Hawk slipped a hat on and started rowing down the canal, while Alex, still decked out in her wetsuit, lay down beneath her blanket. As the oar cut through the water, he belted out the famous barcarola, "Belle nuit, ô nuit d'amour."

"I never knew this side of you," Alex said. "I only wish I could see it."

Hawk tried not to laugh as he continued singing. With a quick glance over his shoulder, he looked back to see the guards at Orlovsky's place calmly patrolling along the rooftop.

One of the guards looked in his direction, but it

was merely a passing glance. Hawk steered the gondola around the corner and out of the guard's line of sight. He tied the boat off at a small dock on the other side of a bridge that connected two central plazas.

When Alex emerged from beneath the blanket, she was no longer wearing a wetsuit, instead sporting a touristy tank top and shorts.

"Impressive," Hawk said to her as they both quickly stuffed their gear into an oversized beach basket and casually joined the flow of tourists.

"Not as impressive as your operatic singing. But like it or not, I have to cross something off the honeymoon bucket list."

"What's that? Swimming in the Venetian canals?" he asked, holding a mischievous grin.

"Uh, no," she said as she shot him a sideways glance. "I was going to say getting serenaded while riding in a gondola. Of course, I didn't imagine me hiding under a blanket while wearing a wetsuit and you being the one doing the singing, but off the bucket list it is."

Hawk stopped and took her by the hand. "You know I'm going to make this up to you, right?"

"Was that ever a question?" she said as she tugged on his arm. "Now let's get this info back to Blunt so we can get back to having fun."

"What? That wasn't fun for you?"

"Hawk, I swear one day I'm gonna teach you how to have some real fun that doesn't involve breaking laws and shooting people."

"I'll welcome that lesson," he said. "Just don't make me dance."

CHAPTER 2

Two weeks later
Washington, D.C.

HAWK PULLED OUT Alex's chair before settling into the one next to her. Blunt was sitting across the table, reading a copy of *The Washington Post* between bites of the chips and salsa situated in the center. After slipping the chip into his mouth, he let out a satisfied grunt once he'd finished.

"Enjoying the chips, Senator?" asked the waitress, who was at least forty years his junior.

"Always, Ella," he said.

"Perfect. Are you ready to order?"

He shrugged. "There's pretty much only one thing on the menu—those delicious fish tacos. Alex? Hawk? You two good with that?"

"Sure," Alex said. "Anything to get food here more quickly. I'm famished."

Hawk nodded his approval at Ella before she bounced away toward the kitchen. He scanned the dive, complete with rustic brick walls and wooden booths. There was even a clunky metal cash register devoid of any digital readout that dinged every time it slid open. Hawk also noticed there were no security cameras or wi-fi. Even the menu was artistically drawn in chalk on a blackboard behind the register. Only a single flat-screen television mounted on the wall served as a lone reminder that this wasn't 1960.

"This is like the place time forgot," Hawk said.

"It's like heaven to me," Blunt said. "You can barely get a signal on your phone here. They don't even accept credit cards at this place. Amazing in this day and age."

"Anything interesting in The Posttoday?" Alex asked.

"A curious drowning by a Russian attaché in the Potomac," Blunt said. "His car careened off the Roosevelt Bridge."

"That takes a special talent to get over the edge of that bridge," Hawk said.

"Apparently, he was drunk off his ass, speeding around in a Ferrari."

"How often do you come here?" Hawk asked Blunt, changing the subject. "You know the waitresses on a first name basis?"

"I come more than enough," Blunt said. "And I've only ever known the waitress as Ella. She was college roommates with my niece, Darcy."

"You have a niece?" Hawk said. "How come I didn't know that?"

"It never came up."

"Well, let's get down to business so we can eat when the food arrives," Alex said.

The television behind Blunt was on CNN. They all stopped talking when the newscaster began a report about Al Hasib.

"Intelligence officials are telling us that following the failed terror attack in London last month that resulted in the death of Al Hasib leader Karif Fazil, the terrorist group has virtually collapsed and no longer poses a threat to national security."

The anchor woman appeared on the screen again.

"President Young, who has been stumping for fellow party senators and congressional representatives on a swing through the southeast, had this to say at a political rally earlier today."

Footage of President Noah Young gripping a podium as he spoke rolled across the television.

"We refuse to cower in fear to these radical groups that have no agenda other than to cause harm to our people," Young said. "The systematic takedown of Al Hasib would've never happened without the dedicated members of this great country's intelligence staff working tirelessly to keep all of us safe and to root out evil in the darkest places of this planet. Because of our intelligence organizations, not only is America safer but so is the rest of the world."

A thunderous applause followed his comment, which led the newscaster into introducing a panel of foreign intelligence experts who debated the veracity of President Young's statement. That inane banter drove Blunt to ask Ella to mute the television so they could have a productive meal without having to listen to people shouting at each other.

Blunt turned toward Hawk and Alex.

"I appreciate all your work in Venice. That was a major coup for us."

"When you say *us*, what exactly do you mean?" Hawk asked. "Our country? You personally? The CIA?"

"Take your pick," Blunt said. "Perhaps, all of the above. But I know what you're driving at."

"What's that?"

"You want to know what team you're on. Who do you report to? Who's going to bail you out if you find yourself in a jam? Who sets the mission parameters?"

"That would be nice to know," Alex said, "that is, if you intend on all of us continuing to work together. In fact, that's vital for me. If I don't know who's in charge—"

"I'm very well aware of what you do, Alex, when there isn't structure in place."

She smiled. "That's what you love about me, isn't it? Just admit it."

Blunt chuckled. "The real irony is that not only are you returning to work for the CIA now, you're going to be doing so as a celebrated hero."

She scowled. "Nobody said anything about working for the CIA. I liked Firestorm. It was the perfect setup for me."

Blunt waved dismissively. "Before you get all twisted up about this, just calm down and hear me out. Okay?"

Alex crossed her arms and leaned back in her seat. "You know I don't like being lied to," she said, glaring at Blunt. "That's why I was more than happy to leave the CIA when they showed me the door. But I expect more out of you. I expect—"

"Honesty? Integrity?" Blunt said, holding his hands out. "Look, we're in the espionage business. Openness and accountability aren't two traits that are high up on the list when it comes to being successful. People by nature are deceitful. Then when you hire one to spy on another person—"

Blunt let his words hang, the implication plain enough.

"*We* can be different," she said. "We can be just like all the other spies when it comes to operating elsewhere, but among us, among thisteam, we need to shoot each other straight."

Hawk nodded in agreement. "I know Alex has strong feelings about this because of her past with the CIA, but I also want to make sure that we're not just doing some rogue bureaucrat's bidding when we embark on these missions. I want to know that we're doing something that matters for America."

"Everything we do matters in one way or another," Blunt said. "But I can assure you that we will be diligent to exact justice and eliminate threats to this country. Is that what you need to hear?"

"Is it the truth?" Alex asked.

Blunt nodded. "I feel the same way both of you do. And I'll be damned if I'm gonna spend my twilight years in this business settling scores between petty politicians. We will do such great work that if anyone actually knew about it, they would be proud of us."

"So, is that what you wanted to talk with us about today?" Alex asked. "I have more questions about this new agency that we're going to be a part of."

"I'll be more than happy to answer anything you want to know, but before we jump into that, I need to tell you a little piece of news related to this."

"Go on," Hawk said. "You know how much we

hate suspense."

"General Van Fortner has just been appointed as the new CIA director," Blunt said.

Alex cocked her head to one side and furrowed her brow. "And what exactly does that mean?"

"It means we have an ally at Langley, an all-important one. And even better than that, we're going to be working on a few cases that extend a little bit beyond the agency's jurisdiction. And all of it will be off the books. No trace of it. No paper trail. Nothing. We're all ghosts as far as it concerns certain missions."

"I like the sound of that," Hawk said.

"Me too," Alex added. "When are we going to start working on these?"

"As soon as possible," Blunt said. "All we have to do is wait for the call."

The payphone just outside the restaurant began ringing.

"Do you hear that?" Blunt asked as he stood. "I need to grab that."

Blunt hobbled outside. Hawk and Alex could see the phone from their position inside the restaurant and both wore puzzled looks when Blunt answered the call. After a few seconds, he replaced the receiver on the hook and returned.

"That was short," Hawk said. "Who was it?"

"It was business," Blunt said.

"Wait," Alex said, holding up her hands. "You mean to tell me that we came to this restaurant not because of the street tacos but because of the old school telephone still attached to the wall outside?"

Blunt grinned. "I hate street tacos. Most over-rated food on the planet. I only come here to give Ella big tips."

"That was a brief conversation," Hawk said. "I'm not sure you even said a word. Care to fill us in on what's happening?"

"We're going to work. That's what's happening," Blunt said.

He stood near the edge of the table and slapped Hawk on the back before yanking him to his feet. Blunt then held out his hand and assisted Alex up.

"You didn't say a word, yet you knew something was afoot," Hawk said. "I'm not sure this is exactly what we had in mind when we were talking about openness and honesty and transparency."

"I'm telling you now, just a few seconds after I found out anything definitively," Blunt said. "You best roll up your sleeves because we've got plenty that needs to get done."

Blunt tossed a one hundred dollar bill on the table.

"Let's go," he said. "There's a terrorist running loose in our city, and it's our job to stop him."

CHAPTER 3

BLUNT DRAPED HIS BLAZER over the back of his chair and put his hands on his hips. With a long, deep breath, he inhaled the smell of fresh paint and new carpet. He paced around his office, admiring the sprawling city skyline just beyond the pristine landscaping on the campus of The Phoenix Foundation.

He strode closer to the window and eyed the organization's sign. The stylish logo with subtle flames leaping out made him smile. When Firestorm was drawing to a close, he reimagined what kind of organization he would start if he could do everything all over again. Those ideas became reality when Fortner called with the news of his impending appointment to head the CIA. And the name was Blunt's clever nod to his past.

Officially, The Phoenix Foundation was a consulting group, another Washington think tank in a city awash with overpaid idea makers. The organization could exist in plain sight, and no one would even question its purpose or existence. To make the mirage more believable, there was a staff, including several former military generals who met with government lackeys about security matters. They also worked with defense contractors to make sure that new weaponry in development was practical in the age of modern warfare.

In reality, the group was a slick way to funnel government funds to a clandestine operation without anyone suspecting a thing. Every year, The Phoenix Foundation would win a large government grant that only it and a dummy corporation was qualified to apply for. Blunt conceived of the arrangement and pitched it to Fortner, who didn't hesitate to help make the set up a reality. As far as Blunt's official title, he was listed as a senior analyst. He had a secretary named Linda who didn't do much more than play solitaire and fetch him coffee in the mornings. She barely looked at his schedule, which contained little more than daily lunch appointments with various people. Also underneath Blunt's command were junior analysts named Brady Hawk and Alex Duncan.

Blunt settled into his office chair and arranged his desk when Linda buzzed him.

"Brady and Alex are here to see you, sir," she said.

"Send them in."

Hawk and Alex entered the office and closed the door behind them. As he looked around, Hawk let out a long whistle.

"Nice digs," Hawk said. "What kind of dirt did you have to unearth to get an office like this with a view like that?"

"I have dirt on everyone, remember?" Blunt said with a wry grin. "Now, why don't you two have a seat so I can catch you up to speed on our first official case?"

"Case?" Alex said. "So, what are we? Investigators?"

"As far as anyone around here knows, you're junior analysts, but technically we'll be confirming any intelligence we receive before taking action. I think *case* is more fitting—until it isn't. Now, have a seat and let's get to it."

Hawk gestured for Alex to sit down first before taking his seat. He shifted in his chair and leaned forward.

"So, what's the job?" he asked.

Blunt opened a file folder and pulled out a few sheets of paper with a picture and corresponding profile. He slid them across the desk to Hawk and Alex.

"You're looking at a photo of Dmitry Krasnoff, a Russian ambassador suspected of murder," Blunt said. "Of course, Krasnoff has diplomatic immunity.

He can be evicted but not tried for murder here. If we find that he's guilty, he gets shipped back to his homeland to be tried there."

"And we know that'll never happen," Alex said.

"Who did he kill?" Hawk asked.

"We don't know if he's guilty for sure. That's why you two are looking into this, but he's suspected of murdering Thaxton Thurman, the son of Florida senator Lon Thurman."

Hawk perused Krasnoff's bio.

"Krasnoff has been spotted near the crime scene of eight murders, and nobody has investigated this guy before?" Hawk asked, his jaw going slack.

"No, there have been plenty of investigations," Blunt said. "The problem is that he's always managed to hide behind the embassy."

"And we're going to do things differently?" Alex asked.

Blunt smiled and nodded. "Yes, you are. You two won't be burdened with the bureaucratic red tape that has entangled all the previous investigations."

"Will we be sending him back to Russia if we conclude that he's the killer?" Hawk asked.

"Yes," Blunt said, "and we'll be shipping him in a body bag."

"As it should be," Hawk said.

"Everything you need to know to get you started

is in that file. If you have any other questions, just ask."

Alex bit her lip as she read over the document. "What about database access? Cameras? Security clearance?"

"You'll have access to everything you need, Alex," Blunt said. "You'll be able to legally get into everything all our intelligence agencies have—CIA, FBI, NSA—you name it."

"And will my access be restricted?" she asked.

Blunt furrowed his brow. "Are you asking because you want to know if you'll have to hack in illegally from time to time?"

A hint of a smile crept across Alex's face. "Now why would you ask me a thing like that? You know I always play by the rules."

Blunt shook his head. "If the situation calls for it, I'm sure you'll figure out a way to get all the information you require."

Hawk stood. "Now that we've settled that, it's time to get to work."

"There's a funeral this afternoon for Senator Thurman's son," Blunt said. "That'd be a good place to start. Thurman will be fired up and willing to talk right after he watches his son get lowered into the ground. Raw emotion will serve you well. Good luck."

Blunt dismissed them both with a backhanded wave.

As soon as the door latched shut, he leaned back in his chair and exhaled. This was almost the life he imagined for himself years ago. By his second term in Washington as a Texas senator, he understood politics were more or less a means to an end. He'd already grown tired of the means. The *end* was all he was interested in. And serving in an oversight role in the intelligence world was a far more direct way to influence outcomes, the kind of outcomes that mattered. Americans would retain their freedoms and be kept safer because of the work that he purposed to do.

He was still smiling when Linda buzzed his phone.

"Sir, you have another visitor."

Blunt scowled. There had been no formal announcement of his employment here, not to mention that The Phoenix Foundation had yet to appear in any media articles. Keeping a low profile was paramount to avoiding the scrutiny of the press. Yet someone had found him already.

"Who's here?" he asked.

"A Rebecca Paris."

"Who?"

"Rebecca Paris. She's a blogger for a website called The Skinny."

"Never heard of her."

"She says she was Lee Hendridge's girlfriend."

Blunt dropped his head and closed his eyes. While he normally held reporters at arm's length, he viewed Hendridge as one of the good guys and still felt a sense of responsibility for his death, even though former President Conrad Michaels was the one who ordered the brazen attack that resulted in Hendridge's death.

Blunt took a deep breath and templed his fingers.

"Sir? Are you still there?" Linda asked.

"Yes, I'm still here," Blunt said. "Send her in."

CHAPTER 4

HAWK PEERED THROUGH his binoculars at the graveside service at Oak Hill Cemetery and watched the small crowd. The funeral downtown at the Cathedral of St. Matthew the Apostle earlier that morning had been packed, but only close friends and family had been invited to the burial. It was also a good gauge for determining who Senator Thurman's allies were. Several high-ranking government officials joined the family graveside, including Vice President Charles Bullock.

"What are you thinking?" Alex asked.

"Now that we're married, isn't that my line?" Hawk shot back.

"No, you're the man. You're supposed to read your wife's mind. Don't you know anything?"

Hawk grinned, keeping Senator Thurman in the center of the viewing frame. "Most people wear dour looks on their faces while attending a funeral, but not Thurman. He looks angry, almost as if he's going to hit someone. His fists are clenched, his jaw set. He doesn't look like someone in mourning, at least not a week after his son has been shot."

"Think it's a good idea to approach him here?" Alex asked. "We could wait."

"Like Blunt said, Thurman's emotions are going to be raw right now. He'll be more open to talking about what he knows while he's still fired up about it. Next week, he might be focused on writing a new piece of legislation. You just never know with him."

"Are you sure about that? We're talking about a grieving father here."

Hawk shrugged. "Perhaps, but Thurman is also a man with aspirations of becoming President."

"And you believe he won't take any time to reflect on the death of his son?"

"Thurman is a driven man. I wouldn't be surprised about anything. But what's it going to hurt to speak with him? If he blows us off now, we can talk to him at a different time." Hawk dropped the binoculars and opened his door. "Come on. The crowd is starting to scatter. We need to catch Thurman before he gets to his car."

Hawk and Alex got out of their car and hustled toward the row of vehicles located near the graveside. Spotting the special government license plate on one of the black sedans, they positioned themselves in front of Thurman's car.

As family and friends got into their cars and drove off, Thurman lingered near the grave with his wife. After a few minutes, he finally headed toward his car. His scowl grew more pronounced when he made eye contact with Hawk and Alex.

"Senator, can we have a minute of your time?" Hawk asked after he introduced himself and Alex.

Thurman ignored them, helping his wife into the car first. Once he closed her door, he spun around toward Hawk and moved inches from his face.

"You have a lot of nerve coming here today," Thurman said. "Who sent you anyway?"

"Blunt, sir," Alex said meekly in an effort to soften up the senator.

"Blunt sent you?"

Hawk nodded but didn't say a word.

"Well, I don't know what you think I can tell you," Thurman said. "I just want the bastard who did this dead. Just make it look like an accident, and get it over with."

"Are you talking about Krasnoff?" Alex asked.

"That guy isn't any more of a Russian ambassador than I am the quarterback for the Miami Dolphins," Thurman said. "He's been spotted at the crime scene of eight unsolved homicides. You two better make sure there isn't a ninth."

"I understand your concern, sir. We're going to do everything we can to bring Krasnoff to justice. But we can't just go around killing people indiscriminately."

"Why not? That's how the FSB does it."

"We're not the FSB—or the CIA or the FBI."

Thurman shook his head. "So, you're powerless is what you're saying?"

"No, I'm saying we aren't bound by standard parameters," Hawk said. "If we need to *take care of something*, we can do it without operating within the confines of a slow-moving legal system that sometimes doesn't get justice for anyone."

"That's why I called Blunt," Thurman said. "I just thought you would be able to operate more quickly and get this thing over with. My family has suffered more than enough over this."

"We understand, sir, but there's definitely the possibility of creating an international incident if we aren't careful," Alex said. "We just want to know if you have any idea as to why someone within the FSB might want Thaxton dead."

"I don't know much, but I heard some chatter from one of my friends on the intelligence committee that the FSB accused Thaxton of stealing intel from his girlfriend's computer. She was a Russian liaison working at the embassy in New York."

"We read the file on this earlier, and there wasn't any mention of Thaxton working in counterintelligence," Alex said. "Was your son working for the agency?"

Thurman's anger vanished for a moment, replaced by a slight smile. "No, not Thaxton. He was barely smart enough to get out of bed in the morning. Between you, me, and the fencepost, the only way he ever escaped from Harvard with a business degree was because of his last name. Thaxton wasn't a threat to anyone but himself."

"Are you talking about the drugs and the partying?" Hawk asked.

Thurman nodded. "He was so caught up in that world that he was never going to hold down a steady job. I even called in several favors just to get him an interview at Preston and Fields Investments. They gave him the job because I'm friends with the CEO, but they didn't let him do anything more important than playing around on spreadsheets all day with accounts that couldn't possibly have been real."

"Where did he meet his girlfriend?"

"Ivana was a piece of work, all cleverly disguised behind her exotic good looks," Thurman said. "You should start with her, because if there's anyone who was in the intelligence field, it was her. Working at the embassy by day, but at night, she was a party animal—

at least that's what Thaxton's body guards told me. She was constantly dragging Thaxton to a Russian dance club—I think the name of it is Mixtura—and keeping him out until the wee hours of the morning. She's the reason he got two DUIs last month."

"Do you think she would speak with us?" Alex asked.

"I doubt she'll give you the time of day, at least not at her office. You might be able to chat with her while she's out partying. But get to her early. The later you find her, the more drunk she will be."

"We'd like to get access to Thaxton's apartment in New York, if you'll consent to that," Hawk said.

"That's not necessary. I had all of Thaxton's belongings packed up and shipped back to us here. They are boxed up in his room at our house right now."

"Do you mind if we look through them?" Alex asked.

"What do you expect to find?"

"Maybe a clue as to who's behind all this," Hawk said. "I'm sure this wasn't just some assassin acting on his own."

"I'm not sure you want to wade into that quagmire. Besides, even if you find out something, I doubt you'll be able to do anything about it. These FSB agents acting as ambassadors are untouchable."

"Nobody's untouchable, Senator."

Thurman sighed. "You two are persistent. I guess you can take a peek. Maybe you'll have better luck than I did. I couldn't find anything that looked remotely suspicious. Just names and numbers, all part of his job."

"I appreciate you giving us the opportunity, sir," Alex said.

Hawk and Alex followed Thurman back to his house. Located just inside the city limits of McLean, Virginia, the senator's neighborhood stood in stark contrast to the bustle of the nation's capital. Serene streets and luscious parks marked the area.

"Every time I visit these neighborhoods, I question my career path," Hawk said.

Alex snickered. "You think you could do what these men do? It'd make you go crazy."

"You're probably right. But still," Hawk said, nodding toward a sprawling Victorian mansion with an estate that he estimated encompassed five acres.

"I know, I know. It's the good life, right? You think that until you learn about all the shit they have to put up with. I don't think it's worth it."

Hawk nodded. "I think you're right—until I think about worming my way along the hot desert floor as I maneuver myself into position to hopefully put a bullet in a guy's head before he gets one in mine. Seeing all this does make me question my sanity."

"Trust me, Hawk, you're not made for *this* life. You're doing exactly what you should be doing."

"But look at that." He pointed toward a red convertible Lamborghini parked next to a Lotus in front of a three-story brick home.

"I'll concede that it might be fun for a day," she said.

"Thank you. That's all I was looking for. I just wanted to make sure that my wife was a normal human being."

She chuckled and shook her head.

"Looks like we're here."

Thurman's car signaled left and waited for the black gate to swing open. From the road, not much was visible of the senator's home. An eight-foot white brick wall surrounded the estate. Only the top story of the house peeked over the wall.

When Hawk followed Thurman inside, Alex's jaw went slack. Set back about fifty meters from the road was the Tudor-style home. A well-kempt garden surrounded the exterior, while the grass was cut short and tight like a golf green. At the end of the drive way was a five-car garage that had an enclosed walkway leading to the house.

"Okay," Alex said, "maybe it'd be fun for a week."

Hawk shook his head and grinned. "So you really are a normal human being."

She shot him a sideways glance. "Don't get any ideas. I still like hacking into computer mainframes and going on global adventures with you. And you know I'll never drive a minivan."

"Famous last words," Hawk said.

They both got out.

"If I have to drive a minivan, don't think you won't be driving one too sometimes."

"If we were to get one for some strange reason, I'd soup it up. It'd be the coolest minivan on the block."

She rolled her eyes. "Good thing we won't have to deal with that problem."

The garage door closed behind Thurman's car, and then he met them by exiting through a side door.

"If you don't mind, please make this quick," Thurman said as he strode toward them. "My wife relishes her privacy, and I know she wants to be able to grieve in peace."

"Of course," Alex said. "We'll get out of your hair as soon as possible."

Thurman led them upstairs to Thaxton's room. Old trophies from youth sports covered the top of his dresser, while ribbons and photos were pinned to the pair of corkboards on opposite walls in his room. Several boxes were strewn across the floor, items haphazardly placed inside without any sense of organization.

"What are we looking for?" Alex asked.

"I want to see his planner," Hawk said.

They both rummaged through the dozen boxes or so until Alex fished one out of the bottom.

"This is it," she said. "It's even got this year emblazoned across the front."

Hawk scrambled over next to her. "Let's look at the last three months. That should give us a picture of what he was in to."

Alex flipped through the pages, but the previous month was missing. "Well, that's odd."

"Make a note of that, and mention it to Thurman before we leave," Hawk said. "I want to know if anyone else had access to this information before it was returned here."

Alex zipped through the pages but couldn't find anything that would indicate he was involved in anything suspicious. She went to close it but felt something crinkle against her finger, something that seemed like it was coming from the cover. "Now this is strange. Feel this."

She placed Hawk's hand on top of the padded cover, and it made the sound of paper crinkling.

"Are you thinking what I'm thinking?" Alex asked.

"I already told you that I can't read your mind," Hawk said with a smile. "It's an ability no man actually possesses."

"Get your knife, and cut out whatever that sheet of paper is inside," she said.

"Not necessary," he said as he slid his hand inside and eased out a sheet of paper.

"Jack pot," she said.

"Not so fast," Hawk said. "We need to open it first."

Hawk unfolded the sheet and spread it out on the ground. It was a list of names, a couple which Alex recognized.

"I think we might be on to something," she said.

"I know that name," Hawk said, pointing to one near the top. "And that one, too. These are all FSB agents."

"But what about that one?" Alex asked as she fingered a name near the bottom.

"He's not FSB. He works in the CIA's covert operations."

"And this woman here appears to have a Scandanavian name."

"I'm not so sure this is just a bunch of FSB agents. Pocket this, and let's get out of here."

Alex complied, shutting up the planner but only after taking a few pictures with her phone.

On their way out the door, Hawk pulled Thurman aside.

"Did you find anything?" Thurman asked.

"Nothing all that earth-shattering," Hawk said, "but we did find a page missing from his planner. Has anyone else had access to all of Thaxton's belongings since you brought it back?"

Thurman shrugged. "The maid, maybe his brother who was home for the funeral."

"And who collected all these things for you?"

"Just my secretary."

"Does she have a name?" Hawk asked.

"Yes, Irina Lopovsky."

Hawk eyed Thurman closely, unsure if he was joking.

"Irina Lopovsky?" Hawk repeated slowly.

"Yes," Thurman said. "Do you know her? She's a lovely lady."

"She also sounds Russian," Alex said.

"Moldovan, actually," Thurman corrected. "She immigrated here at the age of three with her mother."

Hawk eyed Thurman closely. "Don't you think that would be important to know, that your son who we suspect was killed by an FSB assassin had a father who employs a Russian on his staff and entrusted her to gather Thaxton's belongings?"

Thurman sighed. "I've known her and her family for years. She's clean. Trust me. All my employees have been through such a rigorous screening process that they could run for a government office without even a hint of scandal emerging from their past despite the media's best efforts to unearth them. There simply isn't anything there."

"So we should just take your word for it?" Hawk asked.

"Be my guest," Thurman said. "Question her all you like, but I promise that you're not going to find even a hint of what you're looking for. And then in the meantime, your chances of finding Krasnoff will diminish. Is that what you want to happen?"

Hawk shrugged. "We're focused on apprehending your son's killer, but we're also not afraid to turn over any other rocks that we might find along the way."

"I understand," Thurman said. "Now, if you'll excuse me, my wife and I would like to continue grieving in private."

"Of course," Alex said.

Thurman led them to the door, stopping to have one final word before ushering them outside.

"Be careful where you dig," Thurman said. "There might be something you find that's best left alone."

Hawk eased into the driver's seat and looked at Alex. "What do you think?"

"I think we've got a potential mess on our hands, and we better figure out a way to clean it up without anyone else getting hurt," she said.

"Without a doubt," Hawk added.

CHAPTER 5

BLUNT STRIAIGHTENED THEN smoothed his tie before standing up to welcome Rebecca Paris. He hadn't even made it halfway across the room before she opened the door and let herself in.

Lugging a briefcase in one hand and a cup of coffee in the other, she seemed to move effortlessly inside.

"I'm sure Linda could've given you a hand if you'd asked her," Blunt said, gesturing to help.

She ignored him and marched toward his desk. Before having a seat, she set her coffee cup down and flung her other belongings into the other chair.

"I don't have much time," she began as she spoken in a measured tone. "And I doubt you do either since you're such a busy man. So, I'll make this short."

Blunt shuffled back to his spot and sat down, wide-eyed as he listened to Rebecca speak as though she were the one in charge.

"Before we begin, I'd like to issue my condolences to you again," Blunt said. "I never had the chance to—"

"Save it," she said, holding up her hand. "You've had over a year to pick up the phone and give me a call. If you really meant what you were about to say regarding Lee, then you'll do what I'm asking you to do."

Blunt leaned back in his seat, interlocking his fingers and placing them behind his head. "After years of working in Washington, I've learned not to make any promises I don't intend to keep. That policy might run counter to how most successful people in Washington operate, but I'd rather do what I do with a modicum of integrity."

"Nice speech," she said tersely. "But like I said, if you really cared about Lee, you'll put your money where your mouth is and help me out."

Blunt chuckled. "I like you. You're bold and sassy. You should be on television instead of buried on the internet."

She held up her hand and looked aside. "Please. Television reporting is an absolute joke. Editors expect you to spin the story for their target audience. And if you don't, you're relegated to some panel to argue like a bunch of second graders on the playground fighting to keep the fat kid off your dodge ball team."

"You don't mince words, do you?" Blunt said with a laugh.

"I guess you've never read my column, have you?"

"No, but I promise you that I'll be looking it up as soon as you leave. You're a breath of fresh air in a city full of people gasping beneath the weight of a million polluted promises."

She smiled for the first time since she entered the room. "Maybe you should be the writer, or at least you could be a source. The Skinny could use someone with your access to all the major players here."

"I'll have to politely decline," he said. "You don't get to rub shoulders with these people by being a snitch. However, I'm open to hearing what you have to say, so please let's get on with it."

Rebecca took a deep breath and then tucked her auburn hair behind her ears. She reached over and dug out a folder from her briefcase on the seat next to her. Opening the file, she pulled out a few pages and set them on top.

"Lee was terrified of getting murdered for doing his job. Obviously, he had a reason to feel that way. But as a result, he never kept any of his really important research at his apartment. He kept just enough on his computer to write his stories, but he always back them up on the cloud in multiple locations. The real juicy tidbits he uncovered were kept in a file in a fireproof safe at my apartment. He was even so nervous about anyone finding out about us that none of our friends ever knew we were dating."

"For what it's worth, when I read Lee's file after he died, you were never in it."

She nodded subtly. "That's why I'm alive today and in possession of these documents, pages and pages of information related to an investigation he was doing on Senator Guy Hirschbeck."

Blunt's eyes widened. "Hirschbeck died a couple of years ago."

"I know—something I don't think is a mere coincidence."

"Why's that?"

"Lee started digging into Hirschbeck before he died. He got a tip from someone—presumably a political rival who wanted someone else to do their dirty work—about the senator's involvement in a secret government task force."

Blunt shrugged. "It's hard not to get involved in one of those when you're on the senate's intelligence committee. Most of them are rather benign, but the senators keep them hush-hush because they don't want their opponents in upcoming elections to have campaign ammunition."

"The committee Hirschbeck was involved with

proved to be costly for him, but not in the political sense. And based on what went down, I think it's safe to say that it wasn't some benign committee. What he was doing led to serious consequences."

"And what exactly was he doing?" Blunt asked.

"I'm surprised you didn't know."

Blunt sighed. "Look, I'll be honest with you since I can tell you're a straight shooter. Hirschbeck and I didn't really get along. I was operating a secret government program myself—and Hirschbeck wouldn't stop hounding me about it. I grew tired of his relentless questioning about what I was up to. Of course, I couldn't tell him because he didn't have the level of clearance I did. In fact, hardly anyone did. Ironically enough, we weren't doing anything that other branches of our intelligence community weren't doing, but we had a license to operate beyond normal boundaries. Hirschbeck had been a thorn in my side, so I can't say that I shed a tear for him when he died. However, I was surprised to hear about his death. He was a decent fellow and a good politician who looked out for his constituents. But the entity that ordered his death remains a mystery to me, a mystery I'm not anxious to solve at the moment."

Rebecca shook her head. "That's the difference between a politician and a reporter. I won't rest until I find out what happened and get the full story."

"So, why do you need my help?"

"I thought you might be the kind of ally I need in this town to find out the truth about what Hirschbeck was into."

"I don't think Hirschbeck was *that* kind of guy. He was more hound dog than Doberman Pinscher."

"That's not what I'm saying, Mr. Blunt. Hirschbeck found out something, and that's what got him killed. He was being a hound dog and stuck his nose where he shouldn't have. I'm just trying to find out what he knew."

"And how can I help you do that?"

"I thought you'd never ask," she said with a smile. "Now, before Lee died, he told me that he interviewed Hirschbeck, who was interested in bringing to light some nefarious agency working in the shadows of the U.S. government. Lee didn't tell me any more than that, but he did tell me that he stashed tapes of his interviews with Hirschbeck in a locker at Union Station. I've tried to get access to them, but I couldn't find the key in any of Lee's belongings. I went through his apartment, but it had already been ransacked. And since I'm not listed as his next of kin or on his will, the manager at the station refuses to grant me access. I've even tried with a few cop friends of mine, but they didn't want to touch it. For all I know, this could be a giant dead end. Someone may have already found the key, opened the locker, and removed all the tapes. But if they haven't, there's a treasure trove in there that I want to get my hands on. Finishing this story is the only way I can truly honor Lee's death."

"Give me the information, and I'll see what I can do," Blunt said, sliding a pad and pen across his desk to Rebecca.

She nodded and scribbled down the info. "For what it's worth, Lee liked you. He had nice things to say about you, which was unusual. To be honest, he didn't really care for most of the people he dealt with, viewing them cynically. But he was a good man who cared about exposing the darkness in our own government."

"Well, there's plenty of that to be unearthed."

She stood. "Thank you for your help. You have no idea how much this means to me."

Blunt stood and ushered her toward the door. "I'll see what I can do and get back with you as soon as I have something. It might take me some time, so please be patient."

"Thank you," she said, nodding at him before exiting the office.

Blunt closed the door behind her and leaned against it. He swallowed hard.

I need a drink.

CHAPTER 6

New York City

THE FOLLOWING AFTERNOON, Hawk and Alex caught a train to New York to see what else they could learn about Thaxton Thurman's acquaintances and habits. Alex insisted that the more information they gathered about him, the clearer the picture would be regarding who was responsible. If Dmitry Krasnoff was just a trigger man, Alex wanted to know who was calling the shots.

Hawk held the door open for Alex as they both strode into Mixtura, the Russian dance club that Ivana Volkov allegedly dragged Thaxton to on a regular basis. It was barely 5:00 p.m., but the music was already thumping with fast beats and techno sounds. Hawk glanced at two women in the corner vaping and laughing. They both stopped and stared as soon as they made eye contact with him.

"Places like this give me the creeps," Hawk said

in Alex's ear.

"That makes two of us," she said. "Let me see that picture of Ivana again."

Hawk slipped her his phone with Ivana's face plastered across the screen. She appeared to be in her mid-twenties, dark hair cropped around her shoulders with bangs, blue eyes, and a small mole on her right cheek. As he scanned the room, he concluded that Ivana's look was a popular one.

"It's like this place is full of clones," Hawk said.

"The bartender will know her. Let's not waste our time."

He nodded at Alex, signaling permission for her to charge ahead while he hung back.

Watching from across the room, he smiled as Alex went to work. She sauntered up to the bar, ordered a drink, and then casually said something to the bartender. He slid her a shot glass and then nodded toward a table in the corner. She said something, slapped some cash on the bar, and spun around to walk away. The bartender wore a big grin as he gawked at Alex.

Take a picture. It'll last longer.

Hawk admired how smooth Alex was. Her wizardry on the computer often left him in awe but not as much as when he saw her in action with people. Extracting information was her true specialty—and she could do it just as well from a file as from a person.

"That's her over there," Alex said as she rejoined Hawk.

"The one in the red dress?" he asked.

"You got it. The bartender told me that she likes Manhattans."

"Then why don't we bring her one to loosen her up?"

"Sounds like a plan to me."

Alex returned to the bar and ordered the drink. When she came back, they both strolled over to Ivana's table.

"Mind if we join you?" Alex asked, holding out the drink.

"Is that a Manhattan?" Ivana asked.

Alex nodded.

Ivana took the glass and then gestured for them to have a seat. "I guess you can sit for a minute."

She took a sip and then glanced over at the bartender.

"Boris is always looking out for me. I swear everyone in this place must know what I drink by now. Even complete strangers learn my drink of choice. But I suppose you didn't just come here to buy me a drink, did you?"

Alex shook her head. "We're looking into the death of your boyfriend, Thaxton Thurman, and are hoping you can possibly shed some light on who might have wanted to kill him."

Ivana rolled her eyes. "Who are you? FBI? CIA? I already told the police everything."

"We're independent investigators," Alex said. "We're doing this as a special favor to Thaxton's father."

"The senator put you up to this?"

"In a manner of speaking, yes."

"I'm sorry, but I cannot help you. The senator is a despicable man."

"Did you meet him?" Alex asked.

"On several occasions—and I don't think there is a more vile human being on the planet. And when I say that, I do so having met plenty of mobsters."

"But you can't tell us about any of Thaxton's enemies?"

Ivana sighed. "Look, if you want to speak with someone who really knows about Thaxton and might be willing to talk, I suggest you talk to Dmitry Krasnoff."

Alex nodded. "He's also on our list of people to interview."

"Well, you're in luck because he's right over there."

Ivana pointed out Krasnoff, who was seated at a table with three other women, one of whom was sitting in his lap.

"Good luck, and be very careful. Dmitry isn't the friendly type."

Alex and Hawk stood and backed away from Ivana's table.

"You want to do this right now?" Hawk asked.

"Why not? This is as good of a time as any to confront him."

"Fine. Why don't you take the lead? Based on my observation, you might be able to get him to talk more easily than I could."

"I'm not even wearing a low-cut blouse," she said.

"That hasn't stopped any of the men from ogling you from the moment you walked in, especially the bartender."

She flashed a soft smile. "Aww, you're looking out for me, aren't you?"

Hawk shrugged. "I'm just doing what I always do when I walk into a room. Get the temperature of what's happening, search for all possible exits, identify potential troublemakers."

"Don't try to get all macho on me. I think it's sweet—as long as you don't start a fight with anyone over me. You've already won."

Hawk shook his head and grinned. "Just go work your magic on Mr. Krasnoff. I'll be nearby in case you need me."

He found a table against the wall and settled into a chair to watch. Alex approached Krasnoff, who didn't seem interested. He nudged the woman off his lap and gestured for Alex to replace her. Alex shook her head, which apparently wasn't the response Krasnoff was hoping for her. He glared at her and shook his fist. Unsuccessful in her attempt to engage him in a meaningful conversation, she retreated to Hawk's table.

"That went well," Alex said sarcastically.

"He looked pretty upset."

"Well, he's drunk, and he didn't like me turning down his offer to sit in his lap."

"The nerve," Hawk said, clenching his fists.

"Easy now. We still need to get him to talk, which he won't do if you rearrange his face."

Hawk grunted. "How did you know what I was thinking?"

"It's written all over your face."

"Look," Hawk said, nodding toward Krasnoff. "He's getting up to get a drink. I'll see if I can coerce him to join us out back for a little chat."

"Just don't make a scene," Alex said.

Hawk strode across the room and eased right next to Krasnoff at the bar.

"Can I buy you a drink?" Hawk asked.

Krasnoff looked Hawk up and down. "Sorry, but you're not my type."

"No, no, no. That's not what I meant. I just wanted to—"

"Save it. I'm not interested."

The bartender handed Krasnoff two drinks, and he spun back toward his table.

Hawk slipped up behind him and jammed a gun into Krasnoff's back. "I just want to talk. Let's not make a scene."

Krasnoff nodded subtly and acquiesced, setting down the drinks and walking toward the back exit. Alex was already awaiting them in the alley behind the club.

"Oh, so that's what this was?" Krasnoff said. "A little good cop, bad cop routine? You Americans are so pathetic. Perhaps you're unaware that I have diplomatic immunity."

"We're not cops," Hawk said, forcing his gun harder into Krasnoff's back.

"What are you then? CIA? FBI? You still can't touch me."

"Claiming immunity won't help you survive a bullet to your brain. Now we have some questions for you, and you better start talking."

Krasnoff raised both hands in the air in a gesture of surrender. "I'm sure we can work this out, Mr—"

"Hawk."

Kransoff smiled. "How fitting. Here you are, swooping down on your prey."

"We don't have time for your wisecracks," Alex said. "We want to know why you murdered Thaxton Thurman."

"So, that's what this is about. Thaxton Thurman. What a sad young man. All he ever did was spend all his daddy's money while partying away his promising future."

"Why did you kill him?" Hawk asked, pressing the barrel of his gun against Krasnoff's back for emphasis.

"I'm not interested in talking with you about that *situation*."

Alex glared at him. "Maybe you call that a *situation* in Moscow, but here it's called *murder*."

"You're wasting your time," Kransoff said.

The door to the back alley flung open, and three large men lumbered outside, all of them sporting brass knuckles.

"Is this gentleman bothering you, Mr. Krasnoff?" one of the men asked.

Krasnoff nodded. The three men spread out and formed a circle around them.

"I would suggest you and your little woman friend here walk away," Krasnoff said to Hawk. "But I doubt these men are going to let that happen."

"No," one of the men said. "It's too late for that."

CHAPTER 7

Langley, Virginia
CIA Headquarters

SENATOR LON THURMAN FLASHED his credentials to the guard standing watch outside the entrance to the CIA headquarters. The guard studied the documents closely, comparing the photograph on the access card with Thurman's face. After skimming through a few papers attached to a clipboard, the guard handed Thurman's badge back to him.

"I'm sorry, sir, but you're not on any access list today," the guard said.

"Access list?" Thurman said with a sneer. "I don't have to be on any access list. Do you know who I am?"

"I'm sorry for the inconvenience, sir. It's protocol."

"Protocol, my ass. I'm the one that makes sure this place has the money to hire nitwits like yourself who don't even know their government leaders. I'm on the senator's intelligence committee for god's sake."

The guard scowled. "Sir, if you think insulting me is going to let me allow you to pass without a formal request being filed by someone on the interior, you're sorely mistaken."

Thurman narrowed his eyes. "What if I called my friend Director Van Fortner and told him what an asswipe the guard at the gate was to me? How would you feel about me making that call? Because I'm going to do that right now."

Thurman grabbed his cell phone and started punching buttons.

"Fine, sir. Just this once," the guard said as he raised the gate. "Don't let this happen—"

Thurman didn't wait around to listen to the rest of the guard's toothless warning. Speeding along the road leading to the main parking lot, Thurman bristled over how he was treated, even though he knew the guard was simply following orders. But those rules weren't for everyone, especially people like Thurman. He could've called Fortner and requested his name be put on an access list, but Thurman didn't want the freshly minted CIA director to have a chance to brace himself. This was going to be an ambush, straight and simple.

Fortner's secretary put up a weak fight to prevent Thurman from entering her boss's office. Thurman shot her a sideways glance, ignoring her protests.

When he thrust the door open, he found Fortner on a massage table, receiving a pounding from a woman who looked barely in her twenties.

"So, this is how you're spending your time these days?" Thurman asked, gawking at the scene.

Fortner rolled over and sat up, keeping himself covered with a towel. "It's not what it looks like," Fortner said. "I was just—"

"Getting a massage on the clock?" Thurman said with a grin. "That's exactly what it looks like."

"No, that's not what I meant."

Thurman looked at the woman and held up a one hundred dollar bill.

"Thank you for your time," Thurman said, handing the cash to her, "but your services are no longer required for today."

She smiled and took the money.

"Wait," Fortner called after the woman, but she'd already slipped outside and pulled the door shut. He turned toward Thurman. "Thanks a lot. I only get one massage a month, and I stay late to compensate for the time that I lose while doing it. I'm not cheating the taxpayers out of anything."

Thurman strode across the room and settled into the chair opposite of Fortner's desk.

"This is more important," Thurman said. "We have business to discuss."

"The kind of business that can't wait?" Fortner asked, pulling his pants on.

"The kind that I don't want showing up on any official documentation."

Fortner put his shirt on and worked his way down the buttons. "Am I going to regret this, Lon?"

"Of course not. I just need you to handle a few things for me."

"Does this have to do with the Russians and their involvement in Thaxton's murder?"

Thurman shrugged. "Maybe, maybe not. You draw your own conclusions."

"Shoot me straight, okay? I'm a busy man, and I need to tend to other matters if I'm not going to get my stress-relieving massage this afternoon."

"I need to know what you've learned so far."

Fortner sighed. "As of right now? Nothing. I had to work some back channels to get things moving because our agency isn't exactly equipped or trained to handle this type of investigation."

"Are your back channels involving a pair of agents named Brady Hawk and Alex Duncan?"

"Technically, it's Alex Duncan-Hawk now."

"Those two are married?" Thurman asked with an arched eyebrow.

"Just became official a few weeks ago, but I'm sure it won't interfere with their missions. They've been working together for a while anyway."

"But they still haven't come up with anything yet?"

"Not that I'm aware of," Fortner said.

Thurman stood, his fists clenched, and then paced around the room. "We can't let the Russians get away with murder like this on our own soil, especially killing a senator's son—my son."

"Just give it some time," Fortner said. "I know this is all still very raw for you and shocking for everyone else."

"Give it some time? *Give it some time?* I don't want to give it time—I want revenge."

"And eventually, I know we'll exact the kind of justice that you'll find satisfying and hopefully give you closure. But in the meantime, I think—"

"You're not listening very closely," Thurman said with a growl. "We know who pulled the trigger. Let's just take care of it."

"Hawk and Alex are doing the best the can, and when they're satisfied that we've got the right man, they'll take swift and decisive action."

"Perhaps I'm not being clear enough for you. I want that Russian dead twenty-four hours ago. We don't need an investigation."

"Please have a seat and calm down," Fortner said.

Thurman moved back in front of Fortner's desk

but remained standing. "I'm not calming down until I get a promise out of you that you're going to do what I asked and order your agents to move on the actionable intelligence we already have regarding who was behind this."

"Well, Senator, I'm not sure I can—"

"I don't need excuses," Thurman said, putting his knuckles on Fortner's desk and leaning forward. "Need I remind you that I'm on the senate's intelligence committee, the one that makes decisions about who gets to run this agency? I have the president's ear, too. And if I think you're jerking me around about this, I'll take some action of my own. Is that clear enough for you?"

"I think you need to let the professionals handle this."

"It's not easy when they're dragging their feet," Thurman said, standing upright and backing away from Fortner's desk.

"I'll keep you posted on anything our agents learn."

Thurman spun toward the door and stopped once he reached it. He turned back around.

"You better, General. I'll be expecting a call very soon with the news that you avenged my son's murder and eliminated a rogue FSB agent taking aim at American citizens. Anything less will be very disappointing and will result in swift consequences."

Thurman exited the room and stormed past Fortner's secretary. She wished him a good day, but Thurman didn't respond as he charged out the door.

The only thing that's going to make this a good day is news about a dead Russian spy.

CHAPTER 8

New York City

HAWK'S THOUGHTS ALWAYS turned toward protecting Alex when he had found himself in dangerous situations in the past. But this situation was intensely different. She wasn't just a colleague any more—she was his wife.

Hawk's first instinct was to engage as many men as possible and render them immobile. If Alex could hold one of the men at bay, Hawk would then be able to assist her in dispatching the remaining attacker. But things didn't go as planned.

Two of the men grabbed Alex first, each one holding her by an arm. The remaining henchman circled Hawk, gesturing for him to come closer.

Hawk took his jacket off and set it down on a nearby crate, maintaining eye contact with the man. Then Hawk rolled up his sleeves.

"Would you like to fix your hair while you're at

it?" the man asked.

Hawk glared at him but didn't say a word. With a quick glance and head nod toward Alex, Hawk signaled for her to be ready.

Turning his full attention back to the thug, Hawk rushed toward the man, stopping just short to swipe at his leg. Since he was already leaning forward in preparation for Hawk's onslaught, the man went down easily. With a swift kick to the ribs, Hawk took control of the fight. The man moaned as he struggled to get back to his feet. Seizing on the man's weakened state, Hawk kicked the man in the face, which sent him sprawling back to the ground. Hawk waited for the man stand upright before delivering a throat punch. The man staggered backward as he gasped for air, his brass knuckles slipping off his hand and clinking against the asphalt. Hawk dished out one more punch to the side of the man's head, knocking him out cold.

Hawk gave Alex a slight nod—and she understood. With the two men on each side of her still gripping her arms, Alex drew her legs up and smashed her feet into their knees simultaneously. Both men instinctively reached for the area where she had inflicted pain, allowing her to get free. Hawk rushed the man to her left, driving him into the pavement. Grasping him by his shirt, Hawk pulled the man up before bashing his head against the ground. After three hits, the man went out.

Meanwhile, Alex spun and kicked the other man in the face. He fell down but rolled back up to his feet before charging at her. She slid out of the way, sustaining only a glancing blow that knocked her off balance but didn't put her on the ground. When the man made a second run at her, Hawk blindsided him, drilling him sideways. They tumbled downward, landing in a shallow puddle with Hawk on top. The final henchman tried to limit Hawk's arsenal to just one hand, but Hawk reached for the brass knuckles that had fallen off the first man and eased them on. With wide eyes, the man looked up at Hawk. He only needed one punch to put the man to sleep, but Hawk hit him twice to make sure it was a long nap.

When Hawk stood back up, he looked over to see Krasnoff racing down the alley and Alex in pursuit.

Hawk dashed after them, gaining ground rapidly. He passed Alex and a few seconds later caught Krasnoff. Hawk tackled the Russian before dragging him back to his feet and thrusting him against the wall.

"I only said I wanted to talk."

Krasnoff shook his head. "You're wasting your time. I've got nothing to say."

"We'll see about that."

Hawk marched his prisoner down the alley, while Alex ran and brought the car to them. As Krasnoff stood outside the car, he resisted getting inside.

"Don't make this more difficult than it has to be," Hawk said.

Krasnoff held his ground, causing Hawk to lose his patience. With a solid right hook, Hawk rendered the Russian unconscious. With a backup plan to take Krasnoff to a CIA safe house for interrogation if he wasn't initially cooperative, having him unconscious was necessary anyway.

After an hour drive outside the city into a wooded location, Hawk turned onto a dirt road and clocked his odometer. He came to a stop along the side of the road and worked to uncover a swing gate camouflaged by branches and vines. After driving inside and resetting the gate, he navigated down a gravel driveway that meandered along a winding path to a small house that was tucked deep in a hollow.

Alex's mouth fell agape. "Who told you about this place?"

"Blunt did," Hawk said. "We've burned almost all of his hideouts—literally, in some cases—that he had to give up a few locations of the CIA's best kept secrets."

Hawk turned off the car and got out. After opening the door to the back seat, he dragged Krasnoff outside. The Russian started to awaken after his feet smacked against the ground. He gingerly opened one eye and then the other.

"Where are we? You know how much trouble you're going to get in for this? People are going to be hunting you down left and right. You're going to be on the run for the rest of your life. You're going to—"

Hawk released Krasnoff, allowing his head to hit hard against a stump. With a clenched fist, Hawk knelt next to his prisoner and stooped over his face.

"If you don't shut up, I'll knock you out again," Hawk said. "Do you understand?"

Krasnoff didn't say a word, instead choosing to glare at Hawk.

Hawk drove his knee into Krasnoff's chest before digging out a pair of brass knuckles.

"Your comrades left me a little gift," Hawk said as he slipped the brass knuckles on his hand. "I figured there's not a better person to use this on than you."

"Now wait a minute," Krasnoff said, hoisting both his hands up in the air. "Let's not act so hasty. I'm sure we can work something out."

Hawk narrowed his eyes. "If by *working it out* you mean that you're going to tell me everything I want to know, then I'm sure we'll be able to. Otherwise, it's going to be a long night for you."

Hawk snatched Krasnoff by the back of his collar, yanking him to his feet. "Let's get you inside and get on with it."

With some rope Alex found in a kitchen drawer,

Hawk secured Krasnoff's hands behind him and then tied the twine to the chair.

"Do you have to make it so tight?" Krasnoff asked. "I'm not going anywhere. I don't know even know where I am."

"I'll make it tighter if you complain about it again," Hawk said. "I'm showing you a little mercy right now. You better take advantage of it."

"You Americans are all so tough when you gain the upper hand," Krasnoff sneered. "But the moment the tables are turned, you beg and plead for your life like a whiny toddler."

Alex chuckled.

"What's so funny?" Krasnoff asked.

"That's not exactly how I remember it earlier this evening when your henchmen had us outnumbered. Instead of grumbling and complaining, the only sound I heard was heads getting cracked against the pavement."

Alex's retort kept Krasnoff silent for the next minute or so as Hawk set up a video camera to capture their interrogation. Once Hawk finished, he clapped his hands and rubbed them together.

"We're all set now, so let's get started. Mr. Krasnoff, can you state your name and date of birth for the record, please?"

"Am I under arrest for some sort of crime?"

Krasnoff asked. "If so, I need to speak with someone from my embassy immediately. If not, I demand that you release me right this instant."

"None of those things are going to happen. No ambassadors, no early release. Answers to questions get you time off for good behavior. Resisting and stalling will get you plenty of time sequestered here. I'm good with a little R 'n R in the woods for a few days, maybe a week if necessary. I've been due for it since my—well, never mind that. Just know that the only thing that's going to get you out of here quickly will be truthful answers to the questions that I'm about to ask you."

Krasnoff sighed. "Get on with it then, will you? I've got plenty of things to do, things that require my immediate attention."

"Like covering up a murder?" Alex asked.

"I didn't murder anyone. I don't know what you people are talking about. I've never killed anybody, not even accidentally."

"Don't be coy with us, Mr. Krasnoff," Hawk said as he pulled out his cell phone. Here's some footage of you the night Thaxton Thurman was murdered. Just hours after he was found dead, here you are parading around the crime scene and peering into it like you're at some carnival freak show."

Krasnoff shuddered at the suggestion, shaking

his head. "That's not what I was doing."

"Then why don't you give us your version of the story?" Hawk suggested.

"No way," Krasnoff said. "There's no opportunity for justice here. This is a—how do you say it in America?—*a witch trial*."

Hawk glowered at Krasnoff. "It's going to end just like one with you swinging from a rope if you don't tell us what happened."

"What difference will it make? You've already decided that I'm guilty. What else could I possibly say that would change your mind?"

Hawk walked into the kitchen and returned with a manila folder. "Mr. Krasnoff, I understand that you have a wife and two children back home in Moscow. Is that correct?"

Krasnoff froze. He said nothing, but the blank expression on his face let Hawk know the answer to his question.

"Humor me for a moment," Hawk said. "Let's pretend that word gets back to the Kremlin that one of their agents rolled over and told the Americans everything. That probably wouldn't go over so well back home. There would likely be some retribution for such blatant treason, the kind of penalty that would be satisfied only when pain was inflicted upon the perpetrator's family."

Krasnoff remained silent, but his face turned beet red, his anger almost palpable.

"I could just pick up the phone and make a call to spread the word," Hawk said. "A picture of you in custody with some CIA agents might be all I'd have to do to sell this story to someone willing to share it with the FSB."

Krasnoff narrowed his eyes. "Fine. You win. I'll tell you what you want to know."

Alex placed a chair a few feet away, positioning it directly in front of Krasnoff. "Why don't you tell us what we *need* to know, just in case we missed a few things?"

"It doesn't matter what I say."

"No, it matters," Hawk cautioned. "At this point, you still have a fighting chance to survive with no one finding out about your confession. But we need to hear everything for us to get to the point where we agree not to put you in any imminent danger. Is that clear enough for you?"

Krasnoff nodded. "I don't really work for the FSB. My role truly is one of an ambassador. I've never been trained and barely know how to shoot a weapon."

"Then what were you doing at all these crime scenes?" Alex asked.

"A few years ago, someone from the FSB

approached me about working for them. I refused his offer because I don't have time for it."

Alex chuckled. "Is that because of all the diplomacy that takes place at Mixtura?"

"You'd be surprised at what you can get people to agree to while watching Russian women dance behind me," Krasnoff said, a sly grin easing across his face.

"Those aren't details I want or need to know," Hawk said. "Now, please continue."

"Well, someone from the FSB learned that my daughter was trying to get into a prestigious boarding school in Paris and suggested that if I help them, they would secure her a spot. So I agreed."

Hawk eyed him cautiously. "So you *are* working for the FSB."

"In a manner of speaking, I guess so. But they don't pay me a single ruble."

"They're paying you in other ways," Hawk huffed. "There's no need to split hairs about your arrangement. Now, what do you do for them?"

Krasnoff shrugged. "Whatever. You think what you want. I just know that my conscience is clear."

"What an interesting thing to say," Alex said. "But that doesn't answer the question. Remember? Everything we need and want to know?"

After a long sigh, Krasnoff continued. "My *job* is

simple. I visit a site after a purported FSB kill and confirm it. All I have to do is observe the crime scene and
verify the identity of the person there. Anyone could
do it, which is why I don't understand why they came
after me. But maybe one day I'll figure that part out.
In the meantime, I'm just doing what they asked me
to do."

"So, who's the FSB assassin you verify kill shots
for?" Hawk asked.

Krasnoff waved off Hawk dismissively. "I knew
you were going to ask that, though I must admit my
answer will sound a little sketchy. Nevertheless, it is
the truth."

"Out with it," Hawk said.

"Every Monday, the FSB assassin leaves a mark
on a park bench near my home," Krasnoff said. "If
there's only one mark, nothing is happening. But if
there are two marks, then I know there's an assignment. I go to a dead drop location and get the details
in a packet left for me. Then I make my way to the
site, confirm the kill, and file a report with someone
at the Kremlin."

"How often does he kill?" Alex asked.

"At least once every few months, sometimes
more," Krasnoff said. "But there's no science to it if
you're trying to predict when the next killing will
occur."

"No, I'm not interested in that at the moment," Hawk said. "I only want to find this assassin. Is that something you can do for us?"

"As a matter of fact, I can," Krasnoff said.

"Lucky for you," Hawk said. "You just narrowly avoided getting tossed into that fire pit out there after taking a few bullets to your head."

"In that case, let's get out of here," Krasnoff said. "That is unless you want the FSB descending upon this safe house."

Hawk pulled out his knife and loosened Krasnoff from the bindings that kept him tethered to the chair. After jerking Krasnoff to his feet, Hawk shoved him toward the door. Krasnoff stumbled before regaining his balance. He stood upright in front of the door.

"Any shenanigans and you're dead," Hawk warned Krasnoff, pointing the knife at him. "Now, let's go bring a murderer to justice."

CHAPTER 9

Washington, D.C.

BLUNT ZIPPED THROUGH the radio stations in his car, searching for one that wasn't running a commercial of an obnoxious salesman, a tedious political ad, or a local service company with an earworm jingle. Going from one end of the dial to the other and back again, Blunt settled on a public radio talk show. With civil guests holding opposing points of view, he found the program refreshing despite the topic of local education reform being of no interest to him.

As he navigated through the early morning traffic, his burner phone buzzed. Every communication with government officials was prone to be captured and reported through freedom of information requests. However, owning a pre-paid cell with enough minutes to get him through a year helped him give other careful Washington powerbrokers a way to access him without drawing scrutiny.

He didn't immediately recognize the caller's number, which was also likely a secret phone.

"This is Blunt."

"Good morning. This is General Fortner."

"Van, how the hell are ya?"

"I've been better."

"Who's crawling all over your ass this time? FBI? NSA?"

Fortner chuckled. "You know how the system works all too well, don't you?"

"Of course I do. That's why I have this job."

"I wish it was just an agency, but it's worse—it's Senator Thurman."

"Thurman? What's stuck in his craw?"

"Apparently, the fact that his son's murderer hasn't been brought to justice."

Blunt sighed. "The Phoenix Foundation isn't like some magical genie where we just snap our fingers to make problems go away. We might operate outside the bounds of the law, but we aren't reckless in how we go about our business."

"That's not the answer Thurman wants to hear."

"Thurman can stick it where the sun don't shine for all I care. We're working on this issue, but it's a delicate situation. We can't afford to act too hastily."

"I'm not sure caution is a luxury I can afford at the moment."

"Is Thurman threatening you?"

"More or less," Fortner said. "He said his position on the senate's intelligence committee wields plenty of power and he's not afraid to use it if he doesn't get a satisfactory answer soon."

"With apologies to the senator, our team is not going to start an international incident over this. And let's be frank: Thaxton Thurman wasn't some model citizen out there. He was almost always in the news for all the wrong reasons. I'll be damned if I'm going to rile up the Russians over this without having all the facts straight. The man we suspect of doing this might be the guilty party or he might not be. But the day this foundation goes out and exacts justice on foreign nationals—people who no doubt have diplomatic immunity—is the day we get shut down. I'm just not going to let that happen."

"Tell that to Thurman. He warned me that if I didn't take care of the problem right away, he was going to speak with President Young about it."

"I wouldn't worry about that," Blunt said. "I have the president's ear."

"Apparently, so does Thurman. He also helped raise more than fifty million for Young last election. Can you compete with that?"

"I shielded Young from a big scandal and kept him from going to jail."

Fortner sighed. "That might mean something to you, but that's yesterday's news. It won't count for much when held up against Thurman's contributions."

"Just give me twenty-four hours to get you a full update," Blunt said. "In the meantime, tell Thurman that we're zeroing in on the suspect, and once we're satisfied that he's the trigger man, we'll handle the situation quickly."

"And if Thurman doesn't want to hear it?"

"Screw him. Don't let him rattle your cage. You have plenty of people in your corner to counter whatever a grieving and half-cocked senator says to the president. Besides, Young knows you and he likes you. If he didn't, he never would've appointed you this post."

"Okay, twenty-four hours," Fortner said. "Don't let me down."

Blunt hung up and swung a hard right toward Union Station.

* * *

BLUNT STROLLED inside Union Station, toting a briefcase. There weren't any pertinent documents inside, but he'd learned long ago that accessories were important in certain situations. This was one of those moments.

Blunt approached the customer service desk and asked to speak with a manager.

"Can I tell him what this is about?" the woman behind the counter asked.

Blunt, who wore his glasses low on the bridge of his nose, peered over the top of them and cut his eyes in both directions before answering. "Tell him it's a matter of national security."

The clerk's eyes widened before she hustled away, disappearing around the corner.

Blunt looked at his watch as he awaited the return of the woman and her boss. A few seconds later, the woman returned with a bespectacled balding man who would've been better served having shaved his head instead of attempting an ill-fated comb over.

"May I help you?" the man asked.

Blunt nodded subtly. "I hope so, but we need to speak in private."

The man motioned for Blunt to walk around the corner and then led him down the hall to an empty office.

"Let's speak in here."

Blunt sat down on the opposite side of the desk from the man.

"Kyle Court," the man said, offering his hand.

Blunt leaned forward to shake it before settling back into his chair. But he didn't say another word.

"And you are—" Court asked, letting his words hang.

"In a hurry," Blunt said.

"Your name, sir. What is your name?"

"I'd rather not say," Blunt said. "This issue is rather sensitive, and I just need you to help me get into the locker of a deceased man."

Court scowled. "I'm not about to help you if you don't tell me your name. How do I know that you have any right to go inside?"

"I wish I could tell you, Mr. Court, I really do," Blunt said. "The fact of the matter is that I'm not exactly supposed to go around blabbing my name to everyone who asks."

Court's eyes widened. "So you're a spy?"

Blunt put his index finger to his mouth, his gaze darting around the room. He then frowned at Court. "*They* might be watching."

Court leaned forward, speaking in a whisper. "Who exactly is *they*?"

"I've already said too much," Blunt said. "I'm afraid I can't tell you any more or risk putting you in further jeopardy. My mere presence here places you in danger."

Court eased back in his seat before breaking into a slow clap. "Nice performance, whoever you are," he said, "but I'm not about to let you into one of our lockers that belongs to anyone but you. Deceased or otherwise, it doesn't matter to me."

"You're putting thousands of lives at risk if you don't," Blunt said. "How are you going to feel if there's a bomb inside that locker and hundreds die on account of your stubbornness?"

"You'll have to do better than that if you want me to open one of the lockers for you," Court said.

"I don't think I've ever met such a callous man."

"Get out of my office, and don't come back unless you have a warrant."

Blunt collected his briefcase and stood. "You're going to regret this."

Court chuckled and shook his head. "I doubt it. Now leave—now."

Blunt retraced his steps, exiting the office area in a huff. He stopped and looked behind him, unable to shake the feeling that someone was watching him.

CHAPTER 10

HAWK SAT BEHIND KRASNOFF, who was in the passenger's seat next to Alex. Warning the Russian that there was a gun pointed at him, Hawk scanned the park where the assassin was supposed to appear. Ten minutes elapsed since the man was scheduled to meet Krasnoff but had yet to show up.

"Where is he?" Hawk growled.

"I don't know," Krasnoff said. "You can't hold me accountable if he doesn't make the meeting."

"Don't start making excuses," Alex said. "We'll do whatever necessary to catch this alleged assassin."

"Alleged?" Krasnoff said incredulously. "He *is* an assassin. I'm telling you the truth."

"Maybe you are or maybe you're trying to wriggle your way out of this situation," Hawk said. "Either way, someone will be held accountable for the death of Thaxton Thurman. If our mystery assassin doesn't show up and follow protocol, then I'm going to blame you."

"I swear to you, I'm telling the truth."

"Are you a religious man, Krasnoff?" Hawk asked.

"Not really."

"Well, you better get religious fast—and start praying. Your chance to save yourself with this bit of information is slipping away."

"I swear on my mother's—" Krasnoff said before stopping suddenly.

After a brief pause, Alex prodded him. "Your mother's what?"

"That's him," Krasnoff said. "He's got the newspaper folded just like he's supposed to and the hat. It's him."

Alex jammed a needle into his neck when he wasn't looking. Seconds later, the Russian collapsed against the window. She yanked him back toward her side of the car, letting him slump over so he wouldn't be easily visible to anyone passing by.

She got out of her car and casually walked down the sidewalk. Meanwhile, Hawk hustled out of the vehicle and slipped into the park. He found a tree to shield himself from the oblivious public milling around and steadied his arms against the trunk. He took aim at the assassin's neck and squeezed the trigger. A few seconds later, he crumpled over. Hawk then hustled back to his car parked behind Alex's and awaited the next piece of the plan to fall into place.

Hawk watched as Alex rushed up to the man and started yelling frantically for help. Acting immediately, Hawk zipped around Alex's car and drove up near the curb directly in front of the bench where Alex was now kneeling next to the assassin.

"Is anyone here a doctor?" Alex pleaded. "This man needs medical attention."

Just before Hawk could arrive, another man rushed up to them.

"I'm a doctor," he said. "I can help. What happened?"

"I don't know," Alex said, tucking the tranquilizing dart into her pocket. "I just found him here like this."

"Let me see what I can do," he said as he checked for a pulse.

Hawk took a deep breath and pondered for a moment the best way to get rid of the mysterious doctor impeding on their plans. Satisfied that there was a way to navigate this situation, Hawk raced up to the scene.

"Is everything all right?" Hawk asked as he leaned over the assassin and doctor.

"It's fine," the doctor said. "I'm a neurosurgeon at University Hospital."

"Well, I'm an ER doc at Providence right down the street, and I'm on my way to work now," Hawk said. "Why don't you let me take him in?"

"It's not a rush," the doctor said. "He's got a steady pulse. I'm not sure what's going on."

"All the more reason to let me handle this," Hawk said. "I'll get him taken care of immediately and find out what's going on."

"At Providence?" the doctor said with a sneer.

"If you aren't willing to take him in yourself, then don't feign some medical superiority over me, okay?"

"Fine," the doctor said, yielding his ground. "He's your problem now."

The doctor exhaled and put his hands on his hips. After watching Hawk work for a few second, the doc shook his head and rolled his eyes before walking away.

By this point, a small crowd had gathered around them, watching what was happening.

"Move it, people," Hawk said as he scooped up the assassin. He stood and lugged the man toward the waiting car.

A few people clapped as Hawk carried away the guy.

Three minutes later, Hawk was in a nearby parking deck and waiting for Alex to arrive. She skidded to a stop in the spot next to him and then hopped out.

"That went well," Hawk said.

"What do you want me to do with Krasnoff over

here?" she asked.

Hawk held up his index finger, signaling for her to wait. He unbuckled his seatbelt and walked around to the passenger side of Alex's car. After opening the door, he dragged Krasnoff out and onto the ground, placing him against the wall.

"You're just going to leave him there?" she asked.

Hawk nodded. "He'll wake up in a few minutes and be fine."

"Are you sure about that?"

"He'll put the pieces together rather quickly. He's no idiot."

She shrugged. "Whatever. Let's just get out of here before someone sees us."

* * *

THIRTY MINUTES LATER, Hawk hauled the assassin out of the car. He was still unconscious from the tranquilizer dart.

"Sorry I can't be of more help," Alex said. "Moving large objects isn't exactly my area of expertise."

Hawk chuckled. "Don't worry. I've got him."

Hawk dragged the man inside the CIA's underground interrogation facility. The agency owned several throughout the city, but this one was the least used and the farthest from downtown.

After chaining the incapacitated assassin to a table, Hawk retreated to the adjacent room behind a two-way mirror. Alex was sitting at a desk with her computer.

"Got a name for me yet?" he asked.

"He has to wake up first," Alex said. "I need his eyes to do a full scan for facial recognition."

A few minutes later, the assassin started to stir. He opened his eyes and studied his surroundings. Attempting to move his arms, he realized he was tethered to the table. He muttered a few expletives in Russian.

"Got him," Alex announced with a triumphant fist pump.

"Who is he?"

"Nikolay Minsky, a Russian geologist who consults with several U.S.-based oil companies."

Hawk's mouth fell agape. "Living in Washington?"

"Apparently. He's got a work visa from one of the companies he works with, so he's legitimate."

"He must know something about oil to be able to worm his way over here, but he also works for the FSB."

Alex smiled. "Why don't you go find out more?"

She walked over to a printer in the corner of the room and waited patiently as the machine whirred before spitting out several pages. She collected them and stuffed them into a manila folder.

Hawk took the file and marched back into the interrogation room. "Nikolay Minsky," he said as he entered the room. "You're going to wish you'd never set foot in this country after I'm finished with you."

Minsky scowled. "I don't know what you're talking about. I've done nothing wrong. Tell me why you've dragged me here to this—this place. Tell me why my hands are bound to this table. Tell me why you've decided to arrest me for no reason."

Hawk smiled and paced around Minsky. "I'll be happy to tell you all that, but only after you tell me why you murdered Thaxton Thurman."

"Who?" Minsky asked.

"Thaxton Thurman, you know, Seantor Lon Thurman's son."

"I'm afraid I don't understand," Minsky said. "I don't follow your American politics and have tried to keep out them for many years."

"Don't be coy with me. You know good and well who Thaxton Thurman is as well as why you killed him."

"I didn't kill anyone," Minsky said.

Hawk settled into the chair across from his captive. "This isn't a trial, though I will be serving as the sentencing judge once we work through all these questions. The more cooperative you are, the more lenient I will be. Is that understood?"

Minsky nodded. "I still didn't kill anyone."

"Lying will earn you a fate worse than Siberia," Hawk said. "I suggest you start telling me the truth so we can all feel better about how this interview is about to go."

"Interview?" Minsky said with a laugh. He pulled up on his chains to no avail. "You call this an *interview*?"

"Call it whatever you like to make yourself feel better. The bottom line is that you're going to tell me everything or else I'm going to make sure you have a less than pleasant stay during your little remaining time in the U.S."

"You can't make me talk."

Hawk nodded. "You're right. I can't. But I can put the word out that you're helping the CIA and put you back out on the street."

"That'd be a lie. No one would believe you."

Hawk pulled out his knife and slid the blade along the edge of the desk. The razor edge left a mark on the table. "Are you willing to take that chance?"

Minsky said nothing as he stared straight ahead.

"Suits me just fine if you sit there and keep your mouth shut," Hawk said. "All I'll do is cut you loose and shove you out onto the street. I'll bet someone else we want will show up for you. We call it killing two birds with one stone, but I'm sure you've heard of that concept before."

Minsky remained stoic.

"You sure you don't want to tell me how you're contacted?"

Defiant as ever, Minsky didn't flinch.

Hawk's phone buzzed.

"I'll let you think about that for a moment while I handle this," Hawk said, glancing at the cell in his hand.

He eased into the hallway and met Alex.

"I hope you've got something, because this guy isn't budging," Hawk said. "Threatening to expose him clearly isn't working."

"At this point, let's take a flyer on this," she said, handing him a file folder.

"What's this?" Hawk asked as he opened it.

"Pictures of dead Russian assassins," she said. "Someone has taken out two of them in recent weeks. Tell Minsky that we're more interested in the motivation behind the person doing all this and that we can protect him."

"It's worth a shot. Thanks."

Hawk took the folder and re-entered the interrogation room. Minsky was staring down at his hands.

"What trick will you try this time to get me to talk?" he asked.

Hawk grunted. "I know you are well aware of

how the game is played, but let's consider for a moment that the rules have changed."

"What kind of rules?"

"The kind of rules where the assassins are the ones being hunted."

"I don't understand."

Hawk opened the folder and slid a few pictures across the table to Minsky. "Maybe this will help."

Minsky's eyes widened as he looked at the photos.

"Dead Russian assassins," Hawk said. "People just like you. Someone is systematically taking out these men. Now, it's not any U.S. government organization that we know of, but someone is eliminating your fellow comrades. I can keep you safe, but you need to talk."

"*You* are going to protect *me*?"

Hawk nodded. "It's very simple. You tell me how you are contacted and by whom, and I'll protect you from whoever is murdering all your fellow assassins."

"Okay," Minsky said with a sigh. "I'll tell you what you want to know, but it won't be much. Everyone is very much insulated in this process."

"Plausible deniability?"

"I don't know what you Americans call it, but the less we know, the better."

"So, how are you contacted?"

"Every Monday I go for a run in the morning. There is a payphone along my route. I pass by at precisely 5:00 a.m. If it rings just once, then I know there's a job for me. If it rings multiple times, I know there's no job."

"And if there's a job, what do you do then?"

"I visit a dead drop site and collect the details of my assignment."

Hawk nodded. "So, who's calling the shots? One of your so-called ambassadors? An FSB agent posing as some low-level diplomat?"

Minsky laughed. "I don't even know what his voice sounds like. I warned you that there wouldn't be much I could give you."

"What's the address of the payphone location?" Hawk asked.

"On the corner of Calvert and Connecticut, just outside a pharmacy. But I must confess that I haven't heard the phone ring since my last assignment."

"Interesting," Hawk said as he stood. "That should be a sign to you that somebody is taking you out one by one. But you'll be safe in here."

"I don't want to stay in here," Minsky said. "I'd rather take my chances out there."

Hawk eyed him closely. "Unfortunately for you, that isn't a choice. You'll stay here until we get this sorted out."

Hawk exited the room as Minsky shouted in Russian. Alex was already waiting in the hallway.

"Good work," she said. "Now let's keep digging and peel back the layers of who's behind all this."

CHAPTER 11

Washington, D.C.

BLUNT TOOK A BIG GULP of his coffee before getting situated in his chair. He jammed the flash drive into his computer and scrolled through the list of names again, checking to make sure he didn't miss anyone. Once he was satisfied that he'd culled the top enemies from the contacts, he printed out a couple copies. He'd stood to retrieve them from his printer when someone knocked on his door.

Blunt spun around to see General Fortner standing in the doorway. "You know, it's not a good idea for you to be seen in this building."

"Don't worry," Fortner said with a wink. "I used the secret entrance through the back. Only your secretary has seen me."

"You have more faith than I do that she'll keep that a secret," Blunt said.

Fortner sauntered over to the chair across from

Blunt's desk and took a seat. "Casually mention to her that you're all working in the intelligence field and everything you do can be traced or recorded back to the source. Implore her to be careful with what she shares."

"That sounds more like I'm telling her to be more cautious when she dishes the dirt on The Phoenix Foundation."

Fortner waved dismissively. "I doubt she'll see it that way. She likely doesn't think the way you and I do. She'll be a little more trusting."

Blunt shrugged. "You might be right, but next time just give me a little heads up if you want to speak, and we can meet somewhere else. But since you're here, you might as well sit down and talk about something I wanted to show you anyway."

"What is it?"

"It's about the flash drive Hawk and Alex retrieved in Venice from Andrei Orlovsky."

"Good news, I hope."

Blunt huffed through his nose. "It's a mix, to be honest. Good news that we now know who he's been funneling his weapons to."

"And the bad news?"

"A few of the people on the list have been our allies at some point in time, but the name that really jumps off at me is that of Russian oligarch Yuri Kovalchuk."

"The agricultural equipment magnate?" Fortner asked, his voice rising an octave every few syllables.

"Forget about what he actually sells for a moment and consider his availability to move incredibly large pieces of machinery all around the world. Do you think most governments are going to scan every inch of those monstrosities? I doubt our own customs agents would even do that. He could move military grade missiles with ease, and no one would be the wiser."

"Apparently we're wiser now."

Blunt nodded. "But we might already be too late. We just received some reports about activity going on in Cuba that we ought to check out."

"Well, you know I can't send anybody down there, at least not officially."

Blunt pulled a cigar out of his desk drawer and trimmed off the end. He stuffed the stogie in his mouth.

"That's what The Phoenix Foundation is for," he said with a wry grin. "Now, I'm sure you had other items to discuss. So, what's on your mind?"

Fortner shifted in his seat. "I need an update on what's happening with the investigation into the man who murdered Senator Thurman's son."

Blunt sighed. "Look, I asked for twenty-four hours."

"And I gave you that. But that time has come and gone. When I get into the office, Thurman will either be there or he'll be calling, ready to crawl all over me if I don't give him a satisfactory answer."

Blunt's phone buzzed, and Linda's voice came over the intercom.

"Hawk is on line one, sir," she said.

"Thank you, Linda. You're the best."

She giggled and hung up.

Fortner wrinkled his nose. "You don't really mean that, do you?"

Blunt held up his index finger and wagged it. "Don't ever say anything negative about Linda. Without her, I don't know where I'd be, to be honest with you. She's like my lighthouse in a stormy sea."

Fortner's eyes widened. "Are you serious?"

Blunt leaked a cheeky grin before answering the phone. "Hawk, how the hell are ya? I've been waiting for your call. I've even got General—excuse me—Director Fortner in the office here with me. What have you got?"

"I've got something that's going to make you very happy," Hawk said.

"You eliminated the assassin?" Fortner asked, his eyes widening at the thought.

"No, but something even better."

"In this case, nothing is better than the assassin

being dead," Fortner said.

Hawk exhaled slowly, his steadied breathing audible over the speaker. "In that case, I guess I have the *next* best thing."

"Which is?" Blunt asked.

"We have the method and manner by which the assassin gets contacted," Alex said excitedly. "We're going to be able to pull on this string until the whole operation unravels and we find out who we're dealing with."

"That's awfully noble of you," Fortner said, "but we were just hoping to hear that the man who pulled the trigger and shot Thaxton Thurman got a quick trip to the morgue."

"We still have him in possession, but I think you ought to keep that little piece of information to yourself—along with everything else we're telling you," Hawk said. "We think there might be some other folks involved, maybe even some Americans."

"What makes you think that?" Blunt asked.

"Nothing right now," Hawk said. "But we have to do our due diligence."

"Actually, on this case, you don't," Blunt said. "We just want a dead Russian."

"But don't you want to know who ordered the hit?" Alex asked.

"It's probably some Russian ambassador who's

actually high up on the chain of command with the FSB. Ultimately, his identity won't make any difference."

"What if it's someone else?" Hawk asked, continuing to argue about the situation.

"Like a North Korean or Chinese official?" Blunt asked.

Alex jumped into the conversation again. "Maybe. You just never know what you're going to——"

"You're going to find a lot of trouble, the kind that originates at home and is a quagmire to escape," Fortner said. "We're not asking you to raze this ring or uncover some FSB operation existing right here in the U.S. I simply want you to kill the man who actually shot Thaxton Thurman. Can I be more clear than that?"

"I understand your position, sir," Hawk said. "And I know what it's like to have that kind of pressure on you, but we need to carry this out to its logical conclusion."

"And what am I supposed to tell Senator Thurman?" Fortner asked.

"Tell him anything you like," Hawk said. "Do whatever you need to do to get him off your back."

"It doesn't work like that. In order to remain credible, I have to give Thurman an actionable plan. I need to be able to tell him what you're doing so that he understands you're being held accountable and not just blowing me off."

"I would never blow you off, sir," Hawk said. "However, if you must tell him something, let him know that we are still questioning the asset, but we will take care of him within twenty-four hours from now. Satisfied?"

Fortner sighed. "If that's all you can do, that's all you can do. You can't squeeze blood from a turnip. Hopefully, this will satisfy Thurman for now. But it won't hold him off forever."

"I know, sir. We'll move quickly on this, I promise."

Blunt hung up the phone and looked at Fortner with wide eyes. "You know he's the best person to handle this—and he'll get the job done."

Fortner nodded. "I'm sure he will. I just hope he takes care of things before Thurman starts to sully my reputation with the committee."

CHAPTER 12

Fort Meade, Maryland

JUST BEFORE DAYBREAK the next morning, Alex headed north to visit her friend Mallory Kauffman at the NSA. As an analyst, Mallory had access to thousands of records. Requesting particular numbers used to put her at risk when Alex worked for a black ops unit, but she officially had top secret security clearance now. As the result of a perk that came from working for The Phoenix Foundation, Alex was entitled to coordinate efforts with the NSA. And she planned to take full advantage of the approved partnership.

Alex dialed Mallory's work phone to warn her to expect a visitor soon. But Alex's cell phone suddenly couldn't get a signal.

"Every single time without fail," Alex said aloud.

She tossed her phone on the passenger seat, made a sharp turn off the interstate, and headed straight toward the NSA's security gate. A buff guard stood outside, his thumbs hooked in his belt loops as he eyed each oncoming vehicle closely.

Alex rolled her window down and held out her identification card.

"Ma'am," he said, tipping his cap at Alex. "I'm gonna need to see your identification card and driver's license."

"Driver's license?"

"Yes, ma'am. I need to take a peek at it if you intend to pass through here."

Alex sighed, flustered that she thought she had planned for everything to make a smooth entrance but instead had to fumble around for her license.

"It's in here somewhere," Alex said as she dug through her purse.

"Take your time, ma'am. I'm in no rush."

The driver behind Alex laid on the horn.

"You must be the only one not in a rush this morning," Alex said.

"People are so rude," the guard said.

"Here you go," Alex said, handing him her license.

"Cute pic," he said as he studied it.

Alex hated her photo. She presumed everyone did. After all, could anyone look like they have their stuff together after waiting two hours to renew their license? The occasional trip to the department of motor vehicles was enough to make Alex consider selling her car and using Uber permanently.

"I wasn't in a beauty pageant that day," Alex said.

"I know, but that doesn't seem to matter in your case."

Alex didn't mind the guard's flirty nature, but she didn't want to lead him on. She held up her left hand subtly, accentuating the ring on her finger.

"Oh, I didn't mean—" the guard stammered. "I was just trying to make small talk."

The woman behind her blared the horn again.

"Why don't you just hurry up so Miss Tooty-Toot behind me here doesn't have a conniption fit?"

The guard nodded. He scribbled down a few words on the log attached to his clipboard before raising the gate.

"Have a good day," he said.

"You too," she said. "Have fun with Miss Honker."

He rolled his eyes while Alex eased up the window. She wheeled into a parking spot and then made her way into the building. The morning shift was descending upon the entrance as the night crew was streaming out.

Always watching over us.

Alex flashed her security badge at the checkpoint and placed her purse and phone on the conveyor belt.

She strode through the metal detectors and was waved forward to collect her things. After navigating her way through the NSA maze, she found Mallory's office and knocked on her door.

"Fancy," Alex said. "You have a door and everything."

Mallory was sipping on her coffee and nearly spit it out when she turned around to see Alex.

"What are you doing here?" Mallory asked, dabbing her lips with her fingers.

"I thought I'd surprise you this morning and get your day off to a great start."

"No, seriously. What are you doing here?" Mallory said, unamused.

Alex sighed and settled into the chair across from Mallory's desk. "We need your help."

"We? As in you and Hawk? Firestorm?"

"We work for The Phoenix Foundation now, which is how I gained access to this wonderful facility here."

Mallory rolled her eyes. "Work here for a while and you'll see that appearances can be deceiving."

"Well, anyway, I was hoping you might be able to help us."

Mallory took another sip of her coffee. "What do you need help with?"

"A number and phone records. A Russian assassin reported that he gets a call every Monday at a certain payphone and that lets him know whether he's to visit a drop site or not."

"And what do you need me for?"

"I need the number of that phone as well as proof that it was called on the day and time that the Russian claimed."

"You got an address?" Mallory asked.

Alex told Mallory the cross streets and watched as her fingers flew across the keyboard.

"Okay," Mallory said as she pointed at the screen, "here's the number. Now what?"

"Look at all the recent Mondays that someone has called the phone."

Mallory pounded out a few commands on her keyboard. The screen blinked as the unit retrieved the answer.

"It doesn't get called very often," Mallory said. "But it doesn't look like anyone has called for the past three months."

"What about before that?"

Mallory scrolled down the page and then shook her head. "Nope. Nothing. No one is calling during that time according to these records."

"Hold on a minute," Alex said, digging her phone out of her purse.

She dialed Hawk's number and waited while it rang.

* * *

HAWK GLANCED at his cell as it buzzed.

"Did you get something?" Hawk asked as he answered the phone.

"Not exactly," Alex said.

"What do you mean?"

"I mean that no one has been calling that number for at least the past three months. So, the only conclusion I can draw is that our Russian friend has been lying to us."

"Are you sure?" Hawk asked.

"Wake him up," Alex said.

Hawk unlocked the door to Minsky's room.

"Rise and shine, comrade," Hawk said as he entered.

Minsky groaned and rolled over. "What time is it?"

"Time for you to get up and start answering some more questions."

"What do you mean? I thought you got what you wanted."

"Apparently, that's not the case. Seems like you were feeding us a few lies last night."

Minsky sat straight up in bed and jerked on the bindings. He glared at Hawk. "I told you that I was telling the truth."

"That's what you said. But Alex is sitting with

someone in intelligence who has access to every phone record made in the U.S. in the past fifty years—and no one has called the number on a Monday at 5:00 a.m. for at least the past three months. Now, if you want me to help you out, you have to help me out."

"I swear to you," Minsky said, eyes wide and wild, "I got a call on that Monday—and every one since. I'm not making this up."

Hawk sighed. "Well, Minsky swears that he's telling us the truth. Can you ask Mallory to take another look?"

"Sure," Alex said. "I'll call you back and let you know what I find."

"Perfect."

* * *

ALEX HUNG UP and glanced at Mallory.

"Are you finding anything?"

"Maybe," Mallory said. "In fact, I think I've found something here."

"What is it?"

"There were some entries made to this phone, but they've been deleted."

"Deleted?" Alex asked, her jaw dropping toward the floor.

"That's right. Deleted," Mallory repeated. "Someone is deleting them."

"Are you sure?" Alex asked.

"I can't be positive those happened around the time of the alleged phone calls—at least, I can't be positive yet. But I'll do my best to extract that information. It's just going to take some time."

"I would say *take all the time you need*, but I know you. You'll take your sweet time for sure. And sadly, this can't wait."

"I know," Mallory said. "I'm going to work hard to get this to you as soon as possible."

"Good," Alex said. "This is kind of important."

"The fate of the world hanging in the balance, no less, right?" Mallory said with a cheeky grin on her face.

"We're not quite there yet, but we might not be that far off. So, don't take this so lightly."

Mallory made a mocking salute. "Aye, aye, Cap'n."

"This is serious, Mallory. Very serious."

Mallory nodded and put her head down before pounding away on her keyboard.

CHAPTER 13

HAWK TEXTED ALEX and let her know that he needed to pay a visit to Senator Thurman. With local law enforcement plodding along with an investigation into Thaxton Thurman's murder, Hawk realized that he needed to be just as thorough about interviewing all the potential players. And there was something that didn't sit right with him regarding Senator Thurman.

The Florida senator seemed all too anxious to have Hawk put a bullet in the killer's head and bury his body in the woods. In Hawk's experience, most people dealing with grief want to do what they can to move on with their lives. But Thurman wanted to operate at a supersonic speed.

Alex responded to Hawk's text by warning him to be careful. It was trite yet he took the message more to heart now. As much as he hated to admit it, Hawk knew marriage already made him think twice about his approach to certain situations. But it hadn't changed anything. He just considered his actions with an extra measure of preponderance. Deep down, he knew his days of playing cowboy needed to be put out to pasture, though he wasn't sure if he could follow through—even for Alex. For better or worse, Hawk was a clandestine operative, and nothing was going to change that.

Questioning Senator Thurman was risky from the standpoint that he was already exerting undue pressure on Fortner. Thurman was on the senate's intelligence committee and very much aware of The Phoenix Foundation's existence. He also had the power to shutter the covert black ops group by pulling funding. How Hawk navigated the interview was important—and tact wasn't exactly one of his better assets.

Hawk arrived downtown and parked in a garage just off Massachusetts Avenue. When he strode through Newcomb's Diner, the tin bell rattled against the glass door, announcing his arrival to the restaurant staff. A waitress shuffled across the room to greet him and offered to usher him to an empty table. Hawk waved her off.

"I'm meeting someone here," he said.

He scanned the restaurant for Thurman, whose breakfast habit was well documented by Washington media. Perhaps it was the drudgery of covering politics every waking moment of their lives, but reporters seemed obsessed with noting where every senator and representative dined.

Hawk finally spotted Thurman, who sat alone in a corner booth at the back of the restaurant while perusing a copy of *The Washington Post*. He seemed more engrossed in the article than the platter piled high with bacon, eggs, and hash browns.

Hawk didn't say a word as he eased onto the seat across from Thurman. After a few seconds, Thurman looked up before his eyes widened.

"Can I help you?" Thurman asked.

"I'm Brady Hawk, sir. I was wondering if I could ask you a few questions."

Thurman scowled and leaned forward across the table.

"Did you take care of it?" he asked in a whisper.

"We're working on it, but I don't like to act so hastily in a situation like this."

"Situation like this?" Thurman said. "What are you talking about? A man—my son—was murdered. Justice needs to be harsh and swift."

Hawk glanced around the restaurant to see if anyone was paying attention to his conversation with the senator. All the patrons he observed seemed enthralled with their newspaper, phones, or their own conversations with their breakfast companions.

Hawk held his hands up, gesturing for Thurman

to calm down. "We're going to handle it, but this man can lead to an even greater treasure trove of intel for us. You don't just dispose of a guy like that simply because justice needs to be served. Besides, don't we always say that the wheels of justice turn slowly?"

"You aren't part of the American legal system. You're a *damn* assassin."

Hawk shot Thurman a look, one that was easily interpreted. Feeling the fixated stare of the diner across the aisle, Hawk cut his eyes toward the man and scowled. The man looked back at his plate of food and returned to eating.

"Watch it," Hawk said.

Thurman bristled at the rebuke and took a sip of his coffee.

"Now, we're working as fast as we can to determine who's behind the hit that was ordered for your son."

"Who cares at this point? He wasn't actually some paragon of virtue."

"Meaning?"

"He was involved with a Russian woman. And knowing Thaxton, he probably attempted to exploit that relationship in some way."

"So you think she's the one who had him killed?"

Thurman shrugged. "Maybe. It really doesn't matter. We just need to make the killer go away for good and serve justice."

"Assassins are just delivery people, trying to send a message that someone else intended to be received for one reason or another."

"Message received," Thurman said. "Now, let's send one back."

"Why are you so anxious for me to handle this guy?" Hawk asked. "I'm starting to wonder if there's something else you're not telling me."

Thurman looked down at his newspaper but didn't say a word.

"Is there?" Hawk asked again.

Thurman sighed. "Okay, I know this doesn't sound great, but I have to make a confession."

Hawk furrowed his brow. "Why do I feel like I'm about to be blindsided?"

"I know who murdered my son."

"You what?" Hawk asked, his eyes widening.

"I know who the assassin is."

"And you conveniently left that little piece of information out? Are you going to tell me how you knew? Or am I going to have to ferret out that information on my own?"

Thurman glanced around the room before returning his gaze back toward Hawk. "I was having an affair with a Russian woman."

Hawk stared at Thurman, waiting for the other shoe to drop. "And?"

"A Russian woman who was the wife of the assassin."

Hawk leaned back in his seat. "Are you out of your mind? Let's set aside the moral implications of what you did for a moment and focus on the fact that you're opening yourself up to be blackmailed or compromised in some way. How could you be so reckless?"

Thurman shrugged. "I don't know. I just met her at a party. She didn't have a discernible accent, so I thought she was just another lobbyist and—"

"A lobbyist? Do you even hear yourself right now? The notion that you thought she was probably a lobbyist and you were still trying to bed her is unbelievable."

"Where have you been?" Thurman asked. "This is Washington. It's just how things are in this city."

"Senators going to bed with lobbyists? That's a common everyday occurrence?"

Thurman nodded.

Hawk closed his eyes and shook his head subtly. "No wonder everyone loathes politicians."

Thurman narrowed his eyes. "Don't act like you have some moral high ground here. You go around murdering people in cold blood."

"Don't try to lump me in with your ilk," Hawk said. "I'm at least smart enough to know not to put myself in compromising situations if I can help it."

"Don't lecture me. Just do your damn job."

Hawk eyed Thurman closely. "So how did you figure it out?"

"I hired a private investigator to follow her. That's when I learned who she really was—and who her husband was. A friend at the CIA gave me the full rundown on who Nikolay Minsky is and why they suspected that he was working for the FSB."

"And how did you know that Minsky was the one who shot your son?"

"My son was scheming to leverage some information he had on a Russian oligarch into a big payday, an oligarch who has ties to the one of the companies Minsky consults with. This guy leases land to the U.S.-based oil corps all across Russia and other countries around the world. And if Thaxton was planning to blackmail this guy, he wouldn't hesitate to have my son murdered."

"So you were playing a hunch?"

"I knew what Thaxton was up to. I had another PI on permanent retainer following my son around. I had to make sure he never did anything to put my standing at risk. It was an insurance policy for me. I'd always rather be ahead of the media on scandals. It helps me mitigate them."

"Well, like father, like son. Right?"

"Look, I was looking out for my—for *our* best interests. I even warned Thaxton about this, but he wouldn't listen. So after I found out that he was murdered, I put together the pieces and followed them to their logical conclusion."

Hawk chuckled. "Yet, you, Mr. Logical Conclusion, slept with a woman you believed to be a lobbyist without considering for even a moment how you might be compromising yourself? Did logic escape you there?"

"Perhaps," Thurman said with a mischievous grin "You should've seen her—"

"Hey, let's stay focused here. Why all of a sudden did you return to your senses?"

"Self-preservation. I love Washington. I love my job. I can't afford to have any of that put in jeopardy. And it would be if Minsky found out that I was having an affair with his wife. I'd either be subject to blackmail myself or end up just like Thaxton."

"Fine," Hawk said before blowing out a long breath. "I'll expedite this for you, but the danger you face is your own doing."

"I understand, and I'm truly sorry about it all. I cut off communication with my Russian friend as soon as I learned the truth about her identity."

"Well, I'm not here to blow up your campaign," Hawk said.

"That's good because I know how things have a propensity to explode around you."

"I'll let you know when it's done," Hawk said. "But you shouldn't worry. Minsky is in a CIA safe house and isn't going anywhere."

"Excellent. I'll be awaiting word from you that it's finished."

Hawk left the restaurant with an uneasy feeling in his gut. He didn't trust Thurman and wondered if there was more to the story that the senator wasn't sharing.

But Hawk wasn't completely dismayed over the meeting. He'd bought more time for Alex and himself—and Hawk intended to use every second of it.

CHAPTER 14

AFTER REALIZING MALLORY was going to be working on recovering all the deleted numbers for a while, Alex retreated to The Phoenix Foundation offices to do a little data mining. Blunt had alerted her to the fact that there was plenty of useable information on the flash drive she and Hawk had retrieved in Venice, but someone needed to sift through it. And Alex welcomed a break from the grind of the case.

The name Blunt found most intriguing was that of Yuri Kovalchuk, the agricultural equipment magnate. He owned a company named Harvest Master, which incorporated a sickle into its logo. The subtle nod wasn't lost on Alex, but she wondered how many American farmers realized that Harvest Master was a Russian-based corporation, beguiled by the very Americanized company name.

Kovalchuk knows what he's doing.

She cloaked her IP address, rerouting it through

seventeen different countries before hacking into Harvest Master's servers. Gleaning plenty of data on shipments that included dates, times, and merchandise, she shut down the portal to avoid getting caught. If anyone attempted to trace her breach, they wouldn't find her. Alex was a virtual ghost in more ways than one.

Organizing the information into a spreadsheet, she scrolled through the data. After a few minutes, one particular item caught her eye.

Well, now that's an interesting coincidence.

Before Alex could investigate any further, her phone rang with a call from an unknown number.

"This is Alex," she said as she answered.

"It's me," Mallory said. "I found all the deleted files. Someone manually deleted them."

"Is that unusual?" Alex asked.

"Yes. In most cases, it's just a complete wipe from one time to another. But this time somebody systematically eliminated certain entries."

"Strange how that happened."

"But that's not all."

"Oh?"

"Yeah, the phone was rarely used. I know—surprise, surprise. But all of the entries that had been deleted over the past six months were from the same number, except one."

Alex sighed. "And who did that one belong to?"

"Nobody in particular. It corresponds to a pay-phone in Rock Creek Park."

"And guess who lives near that particular park?"

"Let me guess—your top suspect?"

Alex smiled. "I think you could call him that."

"Well, let me know if you find out anything else."

Mallory sighed. "Actually, there is something I wanted to tell you about that I found while scanning some closed-circuit footage."

"Go on."

"I found some images of two U.S. senators meeting with four Chinese navy admirals. But get this—I researched their official public schedules, and neither one of them mentioned this meeting. Why would they be hiding this?"

"Why don't you tell me? You're the NSA analyst. Think about it."

"I will," Mallory said.

"Thanks, Mal," Alex said. "I appreciate your help on this one."

"Happy to," Mallory said. "We'll talk soon."

Alex hung up and jotted down a few notes on her pad. She was anxious to pass along the news to Hawk, putting on hold her research of Harvest Master.

"How'd your meeting with Thurman go?" Alex asked as Hawk answered his phone.

"It went okay. Thurman is an idiot; that much is clear now."

She listened as Hawk recounted the details of his conversation with the senator. When finished, she pressed Hawk for an assessment.

"What do you think now?"

"I think Thurman knows more than he's saying, probably trying to cover his own ass."

"That's par for the course in this town."

"Yeah, well, I don't like it. We need all the facts, especially if we're going to off an FSB agent. I don't mind opening up a can of worms, but I want to know what else is going to be slithering out of them when I do."

"I'm with you on that. We need to do some more digging into Thurman."

"Have you heard from Mallory?" Hawk asked.

"She called me back a few minutes ago."

"And did she find anything?"

"She sure did. There was an untraceable cell number that called at 5:00 a.m. every Monday just like Minsky said."

"So, that much was true?"

"Yep, but there's one exception."

"The Monday before Thaxton was murdered, a different number called that particular morning."

"Belonging to whom?"

"Don't know. It came from a payphone in a Washington park."

"Which one?" Hawk asked.

"Rock Creek. There's still a payphone attached to one of the restroom walls."

"Sit tight," Hawk said. "I'm coming to get you, and we'll go take a look ourselves."

"I'll bet there's a camera there."

"That would make things easier."

"Hang on a sec while I check," Alex said. She clicked away on the keyboard before going silent as she studied the results of her search.

"You find anything?" Hawk asked.

"You're gonna love this. There are three security cameras focused on the public restroom at the east end of Rock Creek Park. I remember reading a while back that several women had been raped there."

"So, extra cameras to curtail any would-be rapists. Smart."

"Lucky us, right?"

"Indeed," Hawk said. "That changes our plans a little. Any idea where all the footage for these cameras is kept?"

"The city's parks and recreation office has a location downtown where they're all stored. But I'm not sure they'll let us look at them."

"What about our Homeland Security credentials?

Blunt made sure we had them for situations just like these. It lists us as employees of the president's special task force."

Alex smiled. "I almost forgot about those. I'll make sure I put my hands on them now."

* * *

THE CRAMPED ROOM in the basement of Washington's parks and recreation office smelled musty. Overhead, an interwoven highway of pipes and wires splintered off near various doors along the hallway. Hawk glanced down at the faded tile, which was chipping around the corners where the squares met.

Hawk suggested Alex knock on the door and enter first in an effort to make sure their first interaction with the guardian of the security footage got off to a friendly start. She rapped on the doorjamb and poked her head around the corner.

"Hello? Is anyone here?" she asked.

Hawk leaned inside to see if the room was empty. A portly gentleman with a wispy comb over was slurping on a straw in an oversized plastic cup. He slowly turned around in his swivel chair, looking up at both of them over the top of his reading glasses that rested on the tip of his nose.

"May I help you?" he asked in a baritone voice.

"Special agent Duncan from Homeland Security," she said, flashing her badge. "We were wondering if we might be able to speak with you about getting a peek at some footage outside one of your park restrooms."

The man stood and tugged on his belt. He wiped his hand on his pants and offered it to Alex.

"Kent Carson," he said as Alex shook his hand.

"This is special agent Hawk," Alex said. "He's tagging along with me this afternoon to help with the investigation."

"Investigation?" Carson asked, his eyes widening. "Was there a murder?"

She nodded. "A little over a week ago. We're just trying to rule out a couple of suspects by matching their alibis."

"And you think my cameras will help you determine that?"

"One of the suspects claims he was jogging in the park and showed us his route," Alex said. "We should be able to see him on one of the cameras if he's telling us the truth."

"Okay," Carson said, settling back down into his chair. "Give me the time and date, and I'll see what I can do."

Alex scribbled down the date and time on a scratch sheet of paper and then handed it to him.

Carson's eyes widened. "Got an early bird here. 5:00 a.m.?"

"So he says," Alex said.

"And the park name?"

"Rock Creek."

Carson nodded. "Give me a minute, and I'll see what I can come up with."

As he pounded on the keyboard, Carson's eyes scanned the screen. True to his word, he located the file in just under sixty seconds.

"Found it," he announced. "Come see if this is what you're looking for."

Alex hustled around to the other side of the desk, joining Carson. She peered at the screen, verifying that the time stamps were correct. Starting the footage at 4:55 a.m., he slowed it down to normal speed. They all stared patiently at the screen, divided into four different camera angles.

"This is all we've got for Rock Creek," Carson said, pointing at the screen. "As you can see, the top two images are focused on the restrooms near the north entrance, and the bottom two are near the south entrance."

Less than thirty seconds later, the bottom set of screens turned into static.

"Is that normal?" Hawk asked.

Carson shook his head. "We just had them all serviced about a month ago. As far as I know, they're in top working condition. See."

He pointed at a bank of monitors on the far wall, framing the same locations.

"Fast forward if you don't mind," Alex said.

Carson obliged, speeding up the footage rate. The static remained on the bottom screen until about 5:05 a.m.

"Well, would you look at that?" Carson said. "Back online and functioning properly."

"Could it have been a power outage?" Hawk asked.

"Nope," Carson said. "We've had that happen before, but they're on the same power circuit. If a portion of the grid went down temporarily, they would've both gone out."

"And these cameras don't have a backup power source?" Alex asked.

"They do, but whatever caused this wasn't due to lack of power," Carson said. "If it was just some sort of weird electrical issue, the cameras wouldn't have still continued to record."

"Well, that's just strange," Hawk said.

"You're not kiddin'," Carson said. "Sorry I couldn't be of any more help to you."

Alex shrugged. "Nothing you can do about that. We appreciate your time, sir."

"Hey, you might want to check with one of the banks across the street from that entrance," Carson said. "They have cameras everywhere and might have captured the person you're looking for."

"Thanks for the tip," Alex said before turning and exiting the building with Hawk.

"Now if I didn't think there was something off about this hit before, I do now," Hawk said.

"Yeah, we're dealing with a serious professional," Hawk said. "We need to be extra careful."

CHAPTER 15

BLUNT WAS READING over some intelligence reports about a potential situation brewing in Cuba when Hawk and Alex strolled into his office. He organized the papers in a file folder and then leaned back in his chair.

"So, how did it go?" he asked. "I'm assuming based on the lack of a phone call that you struck out."

"That would be an accurate assessment, though that's not the entire story," Alex said. "There's much more to it than just the end result."

"Go on," Blunt said.

"Well, we tracked down the one anomaly number that called the assassin and traced it to a payphone in Rock Creek Park," Hawk said. "But when went to view the footage around the time the call was placed, there was nothing but static."

Blunt furrowed his brow. "Was the camera still recording?"

"Believe it or not, it was," Alex said. "In fact, we looked at the corresponding cameras focused on a different area of the park. The timestamps coincided before and after the missing footage—and even during the static. It was weird."

"So, whoever did this was covering their ass to make sure they didn't get caught," Blunt said.

Hawk and Alex both nodded in agreement.

"That also means we're not dealing with a simple murder here," Blunt continued. "This one was calculated, even taking precaution down to the phone call that activated the assassin. Doesn't sound like his usual handler."

"It can't be all some strange coincidence," Alex said.

"But what about that technology?" Hawk asked. "Have you ever heard of such a thing?"

Blunt nodded. "I heard there were some things like that in development, but I didn't know of any that had hit the market yet."

"Do you know who was developing it?" Hawk asked.

Blunt huffed a laugh through his nose. "Who do you think?"

"Colton Industries?" Alex asked.

Blunt nodded. "Bingo. You are today's grand prize winner."

"It doesn't take strong deduction skills to figure that out," Alex said. "I just wish Mr. Colton would finally start playing by the rules if he's going to be working with the federal government so much that he captures seventy-five percent of their available defense contracts."

"That makes two of us," Hawk said.

"Three of us," Blunt chimed in.

"His inability to control who gets their hands on his tech might just be the death of us all," Hawk said.

"So, what next?" Blunt asked, steering the conversation back on course. "Where do you see this investigation going from here? Your twenty-four hours with Thurman is dwindling quickly."

"The guy that manages all the security cameras in Washington parks suggested we check out one of the bank cameras near the entrance to Rock Creek Park," Hawk said. "We stopped by there on our way back to the office and asked them to forward all footage during the fifteen minutes before and fifteen minutes afterward to us. Alex is going to see if she can make heads or tails of it."

"Good luck," Blunt said. "It sounds like your last good lead is hanging by that thread. No pressure or anything, Alex."

"I'll do my best, sir," she said.

* * *

A LITTLE OVER A HALF HOUR later, Blunt was startled by the appearance of Alex at his door. Her hair was a matted mess, appearing as though she'd been napping on a counter. She tied her hair, bunching it up before stretching a rubber band around it in a taut ponytail. Holding a pencil, she stuffed it into the tight strands. But her smile belied her disheveled looks.

"What is it, Alex?" Blunt asked.

"I found something," she said, quietly clapping the tips of her fingers together at rapid speed.

"Can you be more specific?" Blunt asked.

"I was able to analyze the footage from the bank," Alex said.

"And . . ." Blunt said, gesturing for her to continue in his impatience.

"I have an image you need to see."

Blunt grunted as he stood and marched around his desk. But Alex didn't wait for him to make it all the way around. She took off, giddy as she'd ever been for any find she made in the past, streaking right back toward her desk. Still limping, Blunt struggled to keep up. Eventually, he stopped altogether and bent over in an attempt to catch his breath.

"Wait," Blunt said. "I didn't know this was a track meet."

"You're the one who put our offices so far away

from yours," Alex said, putting her hands on her hips. "Don't blame me."

"I never expected to have to race you there," he said before breaking into a cough.

"Are you okay?" Alex asked, her tone softening.

"I'll live," he said with a growl. "Now, let's get moving again so I can see what's so special about this photo."

A half a minute later, they strode into Alex's office.

"I like what you've done with the place," Blunt said as he scanned the room. "It's very eclectic."

"This is all just window dressing," Alex said, gesturing around her office. "The real action takes place here."

She stopped short, just in front of her computer terminal. "Take a look at this."

Blunt peered over the top of his glasses. "Is that who I think it is?"

She nodded.

"Does Hawk agree?"

"Hawk hasn't seen this yet. He had to run a quick errand but he'll be back soon. Regardless, I can promise you he isn't going to argue against facial recognition software."

"Facial recognition matched the image of this man with another one in the database?" Blunt asked, his eyes widening once the answer arrived.

"A 99.98 percent chance that it's a perfect match," Alex said.

"Wow," Blunt said. "Thurman's going to be surprised."

"Probably not as much as you think," Alex said. "Why don't you make the call and deliver the news?"

Blunt sighed. "Of course I'll do it. It's why I get paid the big bucks, right?"

"Better you than me," Alex said.

Blunt picked up the phone off the receiver and dialed Thurman's cell.

"How are things going?" Thurman asked. "I hope your team has taken care of our little issue."

"I wish I could say that was the case, but they're still working on it."

"So, why are you calling me?"

"There have been some new developments in the case that I don't want to talk about over the phone."

"New developments? What kind?"

"Look, I'm going to send over agents Hawk and Duncan to brief you on everything."

"Excellent," Thurman said. "They can find me at my office at the Capitol. I'll be here for the next three hours."

"In that case, they're heading over right now and should be there within the hour."

Blunt hung up and turned to Alex.

"Fill in Hawk about these developments after you find him and then tell him to deliver the news with you. It's show time."

CHAPTER 16

HAWK AND ALEX ARRIVED at the Capitol Building and headed straight for Senator Thurman's office. The activity was rather sparse since there were no debates scheduled and neither house nor midterm elections were looming. Many congressional members returned to their home districts to get a jump on campaigning.

Pausing briefly only to say hello to a few familiar aides, Hawk and Alex reached Thurman's office in less than a half hour after Blunt's call. When Hawk attempted to open the door to Thurman's suite, it was locked.

"What's this?" Hawk asked. "Blunt just told him we were on our way."

"Maybe something came up," Alex said.

"Yeah. I'm sure it did."

A man wearing a suit who appeared to be in his early twenties exited from the office suite directly across the hall from them. Hawk flagged him down.

"Excuse me, but would you happen to know where everyone in Senator Thurman's office went?" Hawk asked.

The man stopped and rolled his eyes.

"That staff never works—and when they do, they aren't really working," he said. "If you want to start eliminating wasteful government spending, just start with Thurman's staff. Those people never do—"

"I'm sorry," Hawk said. "I guess I didn't frame my question properly. I was wondering if you've seen anyone in the office today. And if you saw them leave, where did they go and why?"

The man sighed. "I'm good friends with one of Thurman's aides, and she told me about twenty minutes ago that he was giving them the rest of the day off."

"Is that unusual?"

"Thurman regularly releases the staff but never before lunch. I think there were a few aides who were still stuck in traffic on their commute along the beltway."

"Thanks for your time," Hawk said.

The man spun and walked down the hall.

"This just got really interesting," Alex said. "Why would he leave so abruptly after telling us that he would meet us here?"

"See if you can look up his public schedule today," Hawk said. "A lot of senators will post it on their website so constituents can visit if they're visiting Washington."

"Give me a sec." Alex unlocked her phone and started a series of tapping and swiping. Once she found it, she handed her cell to Hawk. "Is this what you were looking for?"

He took the phone and nodded. "He had a full day scheduled after lunch," Hawk said. "Why the hell would he tell his staff to take the day off?"

"Maybe he didn't want to be bothered."

"What do you mean?"

"Politicians work harder than a one-legged man in a butt-kicking contest," Alex explained. "And if you want to take some time off, you need to give time off to the people who work for you as well. Otherwise, they will send you a barrage of texts and phone calls. Everything that needs your approval or input won't move forward without you. In that case, you might as well not even take any time off."

"That makes sense, but it still doesn't explain his rationale for leaving right now."

"Unless he doesn't want to hear what we have to say," Alex said.

"The only reason he wouldn't want to hear it is if he knew in advance what we were going to tell him."

"Well, we've got to track him down. And fortunately, I happen to work with—and am now married to—one of the best online hounds in the business."

Alex smiled. "You're so sweet, honey, comparing me to a dog."

"Is *online sleuth* better than *online hound*?"

She winked. "That's a far better metaphor."

"So, will I be sleeping on the couch tonight?"

Alex laughed and patted Hawk on the back. "Of course you won't. But you will be giving me a foot massage while I take a bubble bath. A small price to pay, but I'm sure you won't mind."

Hawk shrugged. "Definitely beats sleeping on the couch."

When he looked at Alex, she wasn't paying attention, peering down the hallway as if in a trance.

"What are you looking at?" he asked.

"Isn't that Thomas Colton?"

Hawk turned and gazed in the same direction Alex was looking.

"What's he doing here?" Hawk asked.

"He's got weapons to sell, senators to schmooze," she said. "Want to go say hello?"

"No," Hawk said, "but I have to. It's always good to know what he's up to. And I know he'll shoot me straight."

Alex chuckled. "You've known him long enough

to learn that he thought he was your father but kept it a secret from his family only before learning that he wasn't actually your father. Yet you think he's going to tell you the truth about what he's doing here?"

"I—*we* saved his life. He might be a sleazy legal arms dealer, but he does have some modicum of decency. He's not going to soon forget what we did for him."

"Perhaps you're right, but that doesn't mean he's going to spill the beans."

"He knows better than to keep anything from us," Hawk said. "If he senses that we suspect he's up to anything, he knows we can find out for ourselves what's really going on. The man can keep a secret, but he's a terrible liar when confronted."

"So, you still want to talk to him?" she asked.

"It's always good to keep a pulse on what he's doing, for better or worse."

Hawk and Alex strode toward Colton, who was wrapping up his conversation with a senator and some of his aides by shaking hands. As soon as Colton finished, he turned toward the pair of agents. A big smile spread across his face once he recognized them.

"Hawk, Alex," Colton said. "What a pleasant surprise to see you two here. What brings you to the capitol today?"

"I was just about to ask you the same thing," Hawk said, extending his hand.

Colton shook both their hands as the conversation continued.

"It's just another day at the office for me," Colton said. "We've got some new, exciting technology that we're anxious to show off to some members of the intelligence committee."

"You don't happen to have anything that can obliterate closed circuit TV coverage?" Alex asked.

A wide grin spread across Colton's face. "You know, Alex, I like you. Just straight to the point."

"Well?" she said.

"As a matter of fact, we do. It's called the Silencer 2K. Our functioning prototype right now will only work in short bursts, covering about a mile radius. Pretty cool, huh?"

Alex nodded. "As long as it stays in the hands of the good guys."

"So far only a handful of people have seen it, much less used it. But I know where you're going with this."

"You do?" Alex asked, her eyebrows shooting upward.

"Yeah, you're afraid that criminals everywhere will be able to do away with any type of evidence. However, we're adding a failsafe system to the device so that you have to log in with your fingerprint and a special ID code. A list of all the users who activated it along with date and location will be permanently stored on the device. And we'll be able to track each device with a GPS chip we're placing in them so it would be rendered useless by thieves. If they did use the device, they will be confirming their location and identity while the Silencer 2K was in use."

"And all this technology is active on the working prototype?" Hawk asked.

"Not yet, but those safety upgrades are in the plans."

"Anything else you need to tell us about?" Hawk asked.

"What do you mean?" Colton shot back.

"You know, special long-range missiles, odorless gasses that can kill people, impenetrable body armor, drones the size of sand gnats, new chemical agents—anything really."

"Now that you mention it, I doubt you've heard about our new SubZero missile."

"This is news to me," Alex said.

"Me too," Hawk said. "Care to fill us in?"

"We're in the testing phase right now, but this thing will enable our military to avoid getting into those nasty house-to-house fights in Afghanistan. We can just smoke out an entire village without a shot ever being fired—and from a comfortable distance too."

"You mean, total annihilation," Alex said.

Colton nodded. "It gives us the ability to keep our soldiers safe while eliminating entire pockets of terrorists hiding in abandoned villages."

"How comfortable of a distance?" Hawk asked.

"Two hundred and fifty miles, give or take a few miles," Colton said. "The chemicals it uses are effective in a quarter-mile radius from the point of detonation. We're working on expanding that, but for now, we feel like they're going to be effective for what we need."

"And these villages you speak of, how can you be sure they've been abandoned?" Hawk asked. "Because killing everyone regardless of their affiliation is only going to serve the same purpose that all those drone strikes did—we'll just be radicalizing another generation of young people in the Middle East, further perpetuating the cycle of war."

Colton shrugged. "We have other microdrone technology to determine who's inside these little towns. But ultimately, it's not up to us to determine the morality regarding the usage of the devices. We're in the business of providing the tools for modern warfare. Making peace? That's the job of the diplomats and bureaucrats."

"Who's seen this weapon?" Hawk asked.

"Just a few people at the DoD and some members of the senate's intelligence committee,"

Colton said. "There's nothing to worry about at this point. They've only seen footage of them being used."

"Do you know where they all are?" Alex asked.

"Of course I do. They're all heavily guarded in a secure location at one of my facilities here. I learned my lesson before. Trust me."

Hawk shook his head. "I wish I could have full confidence in you, but this kind of revelation makes me nervous. I just can't help it."

"Relax, Brady. I don't want you to have to put out any of my fires ever again. But if it makes you feel any better, I'll even send over some login credentials for you so you can keep track of them."

"*Them*? How many of these missiles do you have?" Alex asked.

"I brought four to Washington for a demonstration later this week. There are only two other missiles we've constructed to give us six total."

"Okay," Hawk said. "I'm not sure I'll be at ease until I see those tracking codes and can find all of them on a map."

"I'll be sure to do that if that's what it takes for you to have some peace of mind."

"I'd appreciate that," Hawk said as he glanced at his watch. "I'd love to stay and chat some more, but we have to get going, and I imagine you do too."

Colton nodded. "Yes, but I'm glad we got to talk.

Maybe next time we can really catch up with what's going on with you two."

Alex held up her left hand, exposing the back of it to Colton. "We do have a lot more to catch up on," she said. "We got married."

Colton's eyes widened. "Yes, let's plan on talking again soon. I want to hear more about that and find out how things are going."

Hawk and Alex bid Colton a good afternoon and headed back toward their car. Neither of them said a word until they were well outside of Colton's ear range.

"Can you believe that?" Alex finally said.

"I wish I could say I didn't," Hawk began, "but it's amazingly so predictable. I would've been more dumbfounded if he said Colton Industries was simply continuing to produce weapons for the government. But you don't get ahead in that business unless you're constantly innovating and integrating the latest piece of technology into your designs."

"Sadly, I have to agree with you. What's wrong with him?" she asked.

"You mean why does he keep wanting to make money?" Hawk asked.

Alex sighed. "That's not what I—oh, forget it."

"I understand what you're saying. The truth is he doesn't have a conscience. It's how he can make such deadly weapons without considering the consequences. To him, it's just another product he can pimp to the DoD."

"He's going to be the death of us," Alex said.

"I hope you're not right," Hawk said. "But I wouldn't be surprised if you were."

"Let's get out of here," Alex said. "We have us a senator to find."

CHAPTER 17

SENATOR THURMAN ADJUSTED his earbuds and scrolled through the playlist on his cell phone before starting with a slow warm-up jog. He ran several long-distance races every year and always proved competitive, including winning the 50-54 men's division a year ago in the Marine Corps Marathon. His next event was less than two weeks away, so he took the opportunity to get in some extra training. Plus he needed to clear his mind.

With the death of his son still weighing heavily on Thurman's mind, he wanted to pound the pavement and see if that brought him any release from all the inner turmoil he felt. But running was an normal activity for Thurman, one that he knew was an appropriate metaphor for the moment in his life. He simply wanted some time out of the office and away from all the demands of his job. Above all, he didn't want to have the impending conversation with the two

Phoenix Foundation operatives who had warned him they would be heading to his office—at least, not yet.

He cranked up the volume on his phone, increasing his speed to match the rhythmic beats of "Eye of the Tiger." Whenever that song was playing, he felt like he could do anything. Some people needed liquid courage to take certain actions. Not Thurman. All he needed was a few bars of his favorite song to get him in the mood to face anything.

After ten minutes, Thurman had settled into his usual training pace of seven-minute miles. He glanced at his watch.

Not bad for a fifty-four-year-old.

Running in his neighborhood afforded him several amenities that enabled him to train longer and harder. The towering canopies provided by the large oaks planted along the median of the roads shielded him from the stifling Washington heat most days or the rain and snow on others. But the most important element was the iron gate with an armed security guard. Thurman didn't want to be captured by some snooping photographer. Several times in public races, photo journalists snagged pictures, but Thurman was always embarrassed by them. If he intended to run for the land's highest office one day, he didn't want some goofy picture of himself out there for the world to mock and make memes from. And he still hadn't forgotten how goofy President Obama looked while riding a bike. Thurman determined not to make that same mistake, necessitating the move to a secure gated community.

Thurman was already on his third mile when a black SUV rolled up next to him. He couldn't see inside the tinted windows and started to grow nervous when the vehicle slowed to match his pace. In an effort to see if the car was indeed following him, Thurman sped up, darting down one of the neighborhood walking paths away from the road.

When he looked over his shoulder, the SUV was gone. Thurman smiled to himself, pleased that he'd been able to outfox the car's driver.

A minute later, Thurman was still reveling in his victory when the same SUV skidded to a halt next to him.

Great. Now what?

He wanted to take off running again but decided it wasn't much use since the vehicle had circled back around and cut him off.

Thurman threw his hands up in the air. "Okay," he said in the direction of the passenger side window. "You got me. What do you want to do with me?"

Agent Alex Duncan climbed out of the near side of the SUV, while Hawk strode around from the other.

"You said you were going to meet us at your office, Senator," Hawk said. "What happened? We went by there and you were gone. Any reason for that?"

Thurman forced a smile. "I just needed to clear my head, which I do by taking a jog. I can't run through the streets of Washington, as I'm sure you understand."

"That doesn't explain why the rest of your staff also went home," Alex said.

"If I didn't send them home, they would be bothering the rest of my day with incessant questioning. You probably know how that is?"

Neither Brady nor Alex flinched.

"Okay," Thurman continued, "maybe you don't. All I can say is that it is the biggest obstacle to me being able to get work done. If my aides are crawling all over my ass every waking moment when I'm out of the office, I can't get a damn thing finished. Sometimes you just have to walk away."

"Or run, like you were doing just now," Hawk said.

"What are you suggesting, Agent Hawk?" Thurman asked.

"I'm not suggesting anything. I'm simply pointing out the obvious—that you didn't just leave your office to get things done; you came out here to get away from the impending shit storm that's about to rain down on you."

"How dare you attempt to castigate me," Thurman said with a growl. "My son's body is barely cold. I think I should be afforded some time off to grieve whenever the hell I feel like it."

Alex shook her head and then studied Thurman for a moment before speaking. "Is it grief you feel—or guilt?"

"What are you talking about?" Thurman asked, his eyes widening.

"You know damn well what I'm talking about," Alex said.

Thurman was already hot from his run, but there was a different type of warm sensation coursing through his body, the kind he always experienced when he felt rage. He knew exactly where Alex was headed with the conversation, but he needed to know if she was playing a hunch or had evidence.

"I'm sorry," he said calmly. "I don't. I have no idea why I would feel anything other than sorrow over Thaxton's death."

She turned and walked back to their SUV, returning quickly with a file folder. Opening it, she pulled out a few documents and handed them to Thurman. He rifled through the images on the pages before returning them to her.

"Are these images supposed to mean something?" Thurman asked.

"Look at the time and date stamp on each picture," she said, offering the papers back to him.

He showed her his palm and shook his head.

"I'm not into games, Agent Duncan," Thurman said. "You either tell me what this is all about or I'm going to politely end our conversation and continue my jog."

"We know you're the one who called in the hit on Thaxton, your own son," Alex said. "These are images of you that day running into Rock Creek Park a few minutes before a Russian assassin received a call across town, alerting him that he had a job."

"I run in Rock Creek all the time," Thurman said, "especially in the morning before I head to the Capitol Building. It's well documented, so I don't know what you're attempting to prove with all of this."

"I might be considerably younger than you, Senator," Hawk said, "but I wasn't born yesterday. We know what you did. And it explains your desire to expedite matters with the assassin. You wanted us to do the real dirty work for you, expunging all the evidence."

Thurman reinserted his earbuds. "I don't have time for this shit," Thurman said. "Have a nice life."

He turned his back on the pair of agents and returned to his jog.

Less than thirty seconds later, he was on the

pavement, his face smashed hard against the concrete.

"What are you doing?" Thurman asked.

"I'm teaching you how we handle uncooperative suspects," Hawk said before jerking Thurman to his feet. "We have a lot to talk about, Senator."

* * *

HAWK DIDN'T BOTHER knocking Thurman out or even blindfolding him. The debate with Alex was a brief one, though they were divided on the issue. However, Hawk pointed out that Alex mostly just wanted to punch the senator because it would make her feel better. In the end, Hawk's suggestion of handling Thurman less violently won out.

After five minutes into the ride, Hawk was regretting his decision as Thurman protested his treatment. He made threat after threat against them for the way they took him down and forced him into a car against his will.

"You do realize this is kidnapping, right?" Thurman asked. "Not only are you going to lose your jobs once I'm done with you, but you're also going to prison. This kind of behavior is unacceptable on so many different levels."

Alex turned around and glared at him. "You are aware that you are guilty of conspiring to have your son killed. I'm sure that if you ever get your day in court, you'll have a difficult time climbing up to that moral high ground without significant cognitive dissonance."

"I didn't murder my son," Thurman protested. "And I swear when I get out of here, I'm going to make sure you can't even get jobs as mall cops."

"We'll see about that," Alex said.

A few minutes—and several threats—later, they pulled into the driveway of a secluded home just outside the city. Hawk navigated into the garage and closed the door remotely before dragging Thurman inside the house.

He didn't waste any time in restarting his intimidation campaign, which was falling on deaf ears. After having heard enough, Hawk turned around without warning and coldcocked Thurman in his left jaw. Thurman crumpled to the floor. Hawk lugged the senator into the basement and waited for him to regain consciousness.

Alex fished Thurman's phone out of his pocket and connected it to her computer.

"What are you doing?" Hawk asked.

"I'm going to find out where he's been recently, particularly if he ran right by the bathroom in Rock Creek Park where the pay phone is."

"That still won't prove anything definitively, will it?" Hawk asked.

"It doesn't need to. We just need him to think it does."

"Good thinking."

As Alex harvested all the information from the senator's cell, he started to awaken.

"What—where am I?" he asked groggily.

"You're not where you should be, that's for sure," Alex said.

Thurman sat up and rubbed his head. "Where's my—what the—"

"Yes," Alex said, "this is your phone, and I'm pulling all the data off it to make sure you're being truthful with us. I've been in this job long enough to know that not everyone tells the truth all the time."

Thurman glared at her. "You can't do that. Give me back my phone right now. Besides, nothing you get will be admissible in court anyway."

"Who said anything about court?" Hawk asked. "We're just trying to handle justice without all the trappings of the legal system, just like you prefer."

"You still haven't taken care of that assassin who killed my son, have you?" Thurman asked.

"When you're tying up loose ends, it's important to do it yourself," Hawk said.

"It's also important to find all the ends," Alex said. "Apparently, you got a little sloppy—and lazy."

"But don't worry," Hawk said. "We'll make sure that all the ends are tied up neatly by the time we're finished here."

"I kid you not, after I get out of here …" Thurman said.

Hawk set his jaw. "If you make one more empty threat while you're here, I'm going to knock you out again," he said. "And that's a promise."

Thurman narrowed his eyes but remained silent.

"That's a good boy," Alex said. "Now, here's your phone. Why don't you go over a few follow-up questions I have for you pertaining where you've been recently."

"I already told you that I was jogging in Rock Creek Park that morning that you have a picture of me," Thurman said. "I go there all the time. I don't know what else there is to discuss."

Alex took a deep breath, exhaling slowly. "There's this little matter of a new weapon called Sub-Zero."

"What about it?" Thurman asked. "Colton Industries put on a demonstration of sorts for several members of the senate's intelligence committee."

"I know," Hawk said. "We ran into Mr. Colton today when we were at the capitol looking for you."

"So, what about it?"

"Well, I started thinking about why a man would have his son murdered," Hawk said.

"For the umpteenth time, I didn't kill my son."

"Don't try to fool me," Hawk said. "I know politician speak very well. And you're right—you didn't pull the trigger. But we both know you placed the call at Rock Creek Park that led to the Russian assassin shooting your son; that much we learned from the data gleaned off your phone."

"You've got nothing, and you know it," Thurman said.

"Oh, we've got *almost* everything. There's just one question I had as I started to investigate this curious murder: Why? What's the motivation for a father to murder his own son? Now, there are plenty of reasons I could concoct, but I needed to find one that made sense based on all the players involved. And that's when I figured it out."

"Please enlighten us, Perry Mason," Thurman said, sarcasm dripping from every word.

"Your son knew what you were doing, and that's why you had to have him killed."

"That's preposterous," Thurman said. "I loved Thaxton and would never do anything to harm him."

"Again, careful politician speak," Hawk said. "You talk like that so often you're hardly aware that you're doing it. You speak the truth in general terms. You didn't *physically* do anything to hurt him, so you hired someone else who would."

"And again, more outlandish lies. Stop while you're ahead. Quit embarrassing yourself."

Alex moved closer to Thurman, edging less than a foot away from his face. "What made Thaxton willing to turn his old man in? The fact that you stole four SubZero missiles from Colton Industrie,s or the fact that you were going to sell them to some terrorist organization?"

Alex eased away but held her steely gaze.

"Are you done now?" Thurman asked. "I'm tired of listening to this shit."

Hawk paced around the room. "Senator, I'm afraid we're just getting started," he said. "You're in for a long night, especially if you're going to be this uncooperative."

"Like hell we are," Thurman said.

Alex shrieked as Thurman grabbed her and whirled her around so her back was flat against his chest. Neither Hawk nor Alex had noticed the knife sheath Thurman wore around his calf or even considered checking him for a weapon.

The regret was visible on Alex's face, worried lines etched into her forehead as she tried to communicate with him using only her eyes. Even though he wasn't the one being apprehended at knifepoint., Hawk felt how Alex looked. He watched as Thurman slid the blade uncomfortably close around Alex's neck.

Hawk put both his hands out in a calming gesture. "Just hold a minute. We both know you're not a killer."

Thurman laughed, a quick burst the second Hawk stopped talking. "We both know I'm not a killer?" Thurman said. "That has to be the quickest about-face in the history of the planet. One second I'm a deranged killer who murdered his own son; the next I'm perfectly normal and would never murder anyone. So, which one is it, Agent Hawk? Am I normal or a murderer? It doesn't seem like you've left much in between for me to choose from."

"Put the knife down, and we can talk about this," Hawk said.

"Like hell I am," Thurman growled. "You two lunatics picked a narrative and tried to make it fit, like a square peg going into a round hole. I'm not about to let you figure out a way to ruin my spotless public service record over rumors and innuendos, completely devoid of any hard evidence."

Thurman eased backward toward the door. Alex fought against him to get free, but he appeared to tighten his grip each time.

"Easy, tiger," Thurman said. "This isn't like someone holding a gun to your head. You have a good chance to knock one of those free and escape. But a knife? All it has to do is ease its way right around this artery here and you'll bleed out before you can say my name. And that's what you'll be trying to say as you plead for your life. But it'll be too late. So I suggest you calm down before I get put in a compromising situation and an accident happens."

Hawk made a move toward him, but Thurman saw it.

"I don't think so," he said. "Back up and stay there. If I feel threatened in any way, I won't have any qualms about protecting myself and slitting her throat."

"I swear, I'm gonna—"

Thurman shook his head subtly. "Stop making promises you're never going to keep. Agent Duncan here is going to accompany me. If she tries to pull some kind of move, she's dead. If you try to follow us, you're dead. If you call someone and a helicopter hovers over us, she's dead. Any scenario where you don't let me leave in peace with her, she's dead. Can I be any clearer than that?"

Hawk shook his head. "I got it."

"Good," Thurman said. "Now put the keys in the ignition and return to the house. If you try anything—"

"I know, I know. She's dead."

"I'm glad we understand each other," Thurman said.

Hawk went outside and followed Thurman's instructions. Once Hawk returned, Thurman instructed him to remain on the couch until they were gone.

Hawk wanted to charge the senator and break his neck. But that wasn't going to happen as long as Alex was in danger. There had to be another way, and Hawk needed to figure it out fast.

After a couple minutes, Hawk heard the car roar to life, and the two of them disappeared down the driveway. Hawk ran out onto the porch and saw Alex's phone and keys lying on the railing. All he could do was hope Thurman would let Alex go before she got hurt.

Hawk was still standing outside when his phone rang. Rushing inside to answer it, he noticed Thomas Colton was the name on the caller ID.

"How are you doing, Hawk?" Colton asked.

"I've been better."

"Well, maybe this bit of info will help make your day a little better."

"Do you have those tracking codes?" Hawk asked.

"See, I knew this would cheer you up. Okay, I'm going to text them to you along with the instructions on how to log into the site. Just follow the prompts and enter the ID codes on the message I'll send you and you can see where they are."

"Sounds easy enough."

"Or I could just tell all this to Alex and let her do it."

Hawk sighed. "No, I can handle it. Send me what

I need to know."

Hawk's phone buzzed with the arrival of the text messages from Colton. Opening up a laptop, Hawk navigated to the site and followed the instructions. He put his phone on speaker and keyed in the first set of tracking numbers.

"How are you doing?" Colton asked.

"I don't know why you're still listening if you're so sure that everything is fine."

Colton chuckled. "Perhaps I just want the same peace of mind that you want. Is there anything wrong with that?"

"No, nothing wrong with that at all."

Hawk waited for the GPS locator to reveal the location of the first SubZero missile. When the map appeared, Hawk squinted at the screen, unsure of what he was seeing.

"Hawk? Are you there?"

Hawk kept studying the image. "Yeah, I'm here."

"Well, what did you find?"

Hawk sighed. "You're not gonna like this."

"What is it?"

"Hang on a second," Hawk said before furiously entering the next set of numbers. The next three numbers all pinged at the same location.

"Hawk? Tell me what you see," Colton said.

"All four of your missiles are in Cuba."

CHAPTER 18

BLUNT GNAWED ON A CIGAR as he put on his blinker and bulled his way into the faster moving lane of traffic. For his troubles, he received a long honk and a middle-finger salute from the trailing driver. Blunt glanced in the rearview mirror before returning his gaze to the road, ignoring the rude gestures. He used to get worked up over such things, but he'd noticed how he was beginning to mellow in his old age.

I ain't got time to get worked up over getting berated in traffic.

His phone rang with a call from Hawk, and Blunt answered it using the hands-free system in his car.

"How'd it go?" Blunt asked.

"About as poorly as possible," Hawk said. "We severely underestimated Thurman."

"What happened?"

"He took Alex at knifepoint."

Blunt took the cigar out of his mouth, which fell

agape. "You've got to be kidding me."

"I wish I was," Hawk said. "But I watched him put the knife to her throat, holding her hostage so he could escape."

"Where'd he get the knife?"

"Apparently he had one on him," Hawk said.

"Well, I guess we should've figured as much. He's certainly not an advocate for the second amendment. But a knife? I wouldn't have imagined that either."

"It was careless and lazy on my part," Hawk said. "I should've handled him more cautiously. I just figured we'd have our conversation and hold him at the safe house for a few days until we got everything sorted out."

"Anything else go wrong?" Blunt asked.

"Unfortunately, yes. Personally, taking Alex was the worst thing Thurman did. But there's more."

"Such as—"

"He sold four short-range missiles that are armed with weaponized chemicals, deadly chemicals."

"Who did he sell them to?"

"I'm not sure yet, but Colton brought four to use for a demonstration. However, Thurman stole them and sold them to someone, and they're all in Cuba now."

"Any ideas who it might be?" Blunt asked.

"I was hoping you could help clear that up for me. I'm not sure about the situation down there and who they might be wanting to target."

"Florida," Blunt said flatly. "There aren't any other countries those missiles could reach that would make sense if Cuba is indeed the bad state actor here. How far are we talking about here?"

"They can travel two hundred and fifty miles and have a confirmed kill radius of a quarter mile."

"That can still do some serious damage," Blunt said. "And if the navigational system on those things are all that advanced, it could be a precision strike that takes out someone."

"It could cloak an assassination attempt," Hawk added.

"A weapon like that could do a lot of things, most of all sowing fear and chaos. But you're certainly not going to win a battle with just a few of those."

"I think it goes without saying that we need to get those missiles back, but I can't do it without Alex. I need her."

"I understand," Blunt said. "But you need to move quickly on getting her back and that situation under control within the next twenty-four hours. The longer those weapons are outside our control, the greater the chance that we're going to lose them for good."

"Until they come crashing back down on American soil."

"Exactly," Blunt said. "And we can't have that happening."

"I'll do my best, but you'll need to have someone else on standby to go down there if I can't. I'm not venturing down there without Alex."

"Fine. I'll get a backup plan going. Go get your wife back, and keep me posted. And, Hawk?"

"What, sir?"

"Good luck."

"Thank you, sir," Hawk said before hanging up.

Blunt wheeled into the garage near Union Station and parked on one of the lower levels close to the entrance.

Never know when you might need to make a quick getaway.

Blunt got out of his car and entered the bustling train terminal. Union Station was still one of those iconic Washington landmarks that he enjoyed visiting. The attention to architectural detail both inside and outside the building made it an interesting place.

After making his way toward the lockers, he fished out a scrap sheet of paper that contained the corresponding number. He promised Rebecca Paris he'd help her, partially out of his own feeling of guilt surrounding Lee Hendridge's death, partially out of his own curiosity. But upon further reflection, Blunt realized he had nothing to do with Hendridge's death.

Whatever got the journalist murdered had to do with what he discovered.

And Blunt wanted to find out what he was dealing with.

Although Blunt had never been trained as a spy, he'd amassed a few critical skills over the years that enabled him to pick a lock. In most cases, he could get an office door open and sometimes even a deadbolt. But a combination lock, like the ones used in Union Station, presented a much larger challenge.

Blunt took a small device out of his pocket and attempted to slide it along the side of the door, aiming to jimmy it loose. When that didn't work, he put his ear to the door and attempted an old school method of cracking the combination. After that failed, he turned to his last resort—a small laser cutting tool he'd swiped during one of his visits to the CIA's lab.

Using his body to shield bystanders from what he was actually doing, he sliced his way through the lock until the latch finally gave way and the door fell open. Blunt glanced over his shoulder to make sure no one was watching. The travelers hustled past him, none the wiser to who he was, let alone that he was actually breaking into a locker.

The contents inside didn't result in any immediate jaw-dropping discoveries. A shoebox stuffed with a few photos and some correspondence, none of which seemed relevant to what Blunt was searching for. There was a coat and some money, including a fake passport and currency from several different countries. After going through the entire locker, Blunt wondered if there was actually anything there or if Rebecca Paris had simply been attempting to catch him in the act of committing a crime. The possibilities seemed vast, especially in light of the fact that the locker was empty.

Blunt was considering that he needed to move on and get out of there when he reached inside, grabbing the shelf with his hand. As he did, Blunt felt an object attached to the bottom with a piece of tape.

Well, would you look at this?

Blunt carefully removed the small envelope, just large enough to place a key or some other small object inside. Loosening the flap, Blunt emptied the contents into his hand. A flash drive landed in the center of Blunt's hand.

For the first time since he began this quest, his eyes widened and a faint smile flashed across his face.

"What did you find out, Lee Hendridge?" Blunt said aloud.

However, Blunt's victory was short lived. The sound of a man clearing his throat in an effort to get attention jolted Blunt out of the past and back into the present. He turned around and was standing face to face with a Union Station police officer.

"Can I help you?" Blunt asked, slipping the flash drive into his pocket.

The cop eyed Blunt cautiously before speaking.

"Perhaps you can tell me why you were breaking into a dead man's locker," the officer said.

"This locker right here?" Blunt said. "I wasn't breaking into it. I was simply retrieving something for the next of kin after she was denied access to it."

"And you knew the combination, given to you by the man who pre-paid for this locker?"

Blunt nodded, attempting to bluff his way past the officer. But the officer wasn't having any of it.

"So, why is there footage on one of our security cameras of you wielding a small laser cutter and ripping through the lock?" the guard asked.

Blunt shrugged. "I have no idea. Maybe someone was trying to plant evidence on me. I am a famous Washington politician, by the way. There's always someone trying to frame me and get me locked up."

"*Former* politician, Mr. Blunt," the security guard said.

Blunt smiled. "So you do know who I am?"

"Yes, I know you faked your own death and you've been instrumental in perpetuating conflicts in the Middle East," the officer said. "I know exactly who you are."

"You're a big fan, I see."

The officer rolled his eyes. "Turn around, Mr. Blunt, and put your hands behind your back."

"What for?" Blunt asked.

"I'm placing you under arrest for breaking into and the destruction of private property. I know you know better."

"There's an explanation for all of this," Blunt said. "This isn't necessary. I haven't taken a thing."

Snatching his hands, the officer cuffed Blunt before digging into his pockets.

"Didn't take a thing?" the officer asked as he held up the memory device.

"I already had that in my pocket."

"In that case you have nothing to worry about since this entire incident was captured on security footage," the officer said, pointing to the camera in the corner of the room.

"You're making a big mistake," Blunt said.

"Tell it to the judge."

Blunt sighed and trudged along at the prodding of the arresting officer.

CHAPTER 19

WITHOUT A VEHICLE, Hawk was stranded at the CIA safe house until he could get someone to pick him up. He considered calling the FBI and letting them know what was going on with Senator Thurman, but that would result in hours of interviews, time Hawk didn't have with four missiles sitting in Cuba. For all he knew, they could be armed and aimed at Miami. Thurman could wait.

Hawk gathered all of Alex's computers along with her cell phone and crammed it into a backpack. In an effort to protect the location of the house, Hawk walked a half-mile down the road before calling Mallory Kauffman and asking her to pick him up. She told him she would be there in thirty minutes and could give him a lift back to The Phoenix Foundation.

While Hawk was waiting, he considered what Thurman's end game might be. Was the senator involved in a far more sinister plot? Was he selling secrets to foreign entities? Was he using the excuse of the weapons as a way to increase spending to the defense budget? Whatever the reason, Hawk determined it was treasonous, certainly not in the best interest of the United States. To Hawk, the most benign action Thurman could be taking was something related to padding his own bank account, but at the cost of the American people. At its most nefarious, Thurman was selling out his country. Or maybe it was something worse, something Hawk hadn't yet conceived possible.

When Mallory's car finally appeared over the rise in the distance, she was flashing her lights and honking her horn.

What the hell?

Mallory skidded to a stop on the opposite side of the street and motioned for him to get inside. He instantly noticed she wasn't alone.

"Alex!" he said, stunned. "How did you—"

Alex opened the door and got out. "Get in, and I'll tell you everything," she said before switching to the back seat.

Hawk hustled over to the car and got inside. Mallory didn't wait for him to buckle his seatbelt, shoving her foot on the gas as she got off to a screeching start.

"What are you doing here?" Hawk asked.

"Before I tell you everything, I think you should know that we're headed straight to the airport," Alex said. "We have a plane fueled and waiting to take us to Cuba."

"Did you talk to Blunt?" he asked.

"No. I tried calling him on Mallory's phone, but I couldn't reach him. I just had Linda authorize everything for us. She even has dossiers on the plane containing our new legends that will enable us to get into the country. I would've called you sooner, but I needed to get all that moving as soon as possible if we're going to have a chance of getting those missiles before they disappear on the black market or are fired at the U.S."

"I understand," Hawk said, though he wasn't sure he would've done the same thing. Calling Alex would've been his first priority, as it always was on his missions. Why she hadn't done the same bothered him more than he wanted to admit.

"Country first, right?" Alex asked.

Hawk forced a smile. "Always."

It was a weak affirmation, his dour expression betraying his words.

"Are you all right?" Alex asked.

He sighed. "I'm fine. Let's just go track down those missiles."

* * *

HAWK SLUNG HIS GEAR onto the plane and then tossed Alex's equipment inside as well. Once they both secured all their bags, they buckled up and prepared for the takeoff. The sun was just rising over the horizon, painting a sunrise with red, orange, and purple hues.

"Where is this place we're going in Cuba again?" Hawk asked.

"The resort town of Varadero," Alex said. "It's quite nice, actually. If we weren't going there to capture some weapons, we could stay a while and get the rest of our honeymoon in."

"Country first, right?" Hawk said.

Alex eyed him closely. "What's eating you? Ever since we picked you up, you've been in a mood. Did I say something?"

Hawk shook his head but remained quiet.

"Did I do something?" she asked again.

"Look, I just would've appreciated a quick call or a text message—anything to let me know you were okay. Do you realize how much that was eating me up? It's not like we're just two operatives working on a mission. You're my *wife*. I'm going to defend you no matter what."

"Hawk, every once in a while that hardened exterior of yours cracks. And what leaks out is surprising tenderness."

Hawk forced a laugh. "I'm not trying to impress you. This is how I feel. It's why I wanted to marry you.

I've never met another woman that I could seriously consider growing old with, especially one who actually enjoys the thrill of these missions and doesn't mind me going on them, let alone joining me."

"And that's exactly why I thought you wouldn't care who I called first," Alex said. "But trust me when I say this—my feelings for you are mutual."

Hawk leaned over and kissed her just as the plane began to rumble down the runway. "I'm sorry I was careless back there with Thurman," he said, settling back into his seat as the plane lurched skyward. "If something would've happened to you, I never would've forgiven myself."

"We both were," she said. "It wasn't just your fault. But you probably could've gone after him, and he wouldn't have done a damn thing to me. You should've seen the look in his eyes. He was terrified. There's a reason why he hired someone else to kill his son, because he doesn't have the constitution for it."

"So, he just let you go?" Hawk asked.

"He drove for a couple miles off the main road and then told me to get out. He did a quick U-turn and sped off toward the highway. I walked back in the same direction and flagged down Mallory when I recognized her vehicle."

"How could you miss it?" Hawk asked.

"A yellow convertible VW bug. It's hard to miss."

"You don't think Thurman had any intention of hurting you?" Hawk asked.

"No, he was more scared than I was. For a brief moment, I considered attacking him, but I decided to see how things played out. It was too big of a risk. It's not like he's going to disappear forever. We'll track him down."

"And he's going to pay—one way or another."

Alex nodded in agreement before opening up her laptop. She keyed in the tracking codes for the Sub-Zero missiles.

"Are they all still there?" Hawk asked.

"The first three are," she said. "Just one more to check." Alex entered the final numbers and pressed enter. "Yep. They're all there."

"Can you pinpoint the address for them all?" Hawk asked.

"I've got GPS coordinates for all four missiles, and they seem to be clustered together."

"That should be easy enough, barring any problems."

She chuckled. "Yes, because nothing ever goes wrong."

"That's right. I'm sure you've already concocted a fool-proof plan."

"Of course I have."

Hawk's eyebrows shot upward. "You know

exactly where all the missiles are being held?"

She nodded. "Varadero Azul Hotel. I'm not sure the floor yet, but I'll be able to set off a homing beacon that will take us right to the spot once we're in the vicinity. Colton sent me instructions on how to operate that as well through my cell phone."

"So, what's this big plan of yours?" Hawk asked.

"You're going to be a concierge."

* * *

WHEN HAWK AND ALEX landed in Varadero, they breezed through customs, posing as a banker from Zurich along with his assistant to discuss investment options in the Caymans with a resort owner. They kept the details vague with the customs agent, who didn't seem too interested in prolonging their visit to his kiosk.

Hawk and Alex spent over an hour trying to rent a car before driving straight to their hotel and getting to work. By the time they set up their command post in their hotel room and secured all the supplies they needed, it was getting late. Whoever was in possession of the missiles might be returning back from dinner soon. The less resistance, the better.

With a room on the eleventh floor, Hawk and Alex could see the entire peninsula where vacationers relaxed on the beach while the sea lapped gently against the shore. The sun had already started to dip below the horizon. Alex sauntered over to the window and stared out into the distance. Hawk put his arm around her.

"Wouldn't it be nice to be out there, stretched out on the beach, reading a novel?" Hawk asked.

Alex shook her head. "That's not the life we chose—or even one we'd be satisfied with, and you know it. Making sure people can enjoy their day at the beach—that's what we do. And we love it. Don't even try to deny it."

"Sure, but sometimes don't you just think—"

"The grass is always greener, especially when you don't have to mow it."

Hawk chuckled. "Where'd you come up with that one? Fortune cookie?"

Alex smiled. "No, the latest Salman Kahn movie."

"He has the best lines, doesn't he?"

"Well, if we're only talking about Bollywood films, then yes."

Hawk laughed. "Let's finish this so we can go find a beach somewhere."

A half hour later, Hawk was suited up in a concierge uniform he'd stolen from the laundry room. He also found a stray cart with leftover food from a room service order parked outside someone's door. Hawk claimed the cart and wheeled it back to his room.

"What do I need to do to make this work?" Hawk asked.

"The homing beacon has been activated as of twenty seconds ago," Alex said. "Just use the app I installed on your phone to find it. Your screen should give you a 3D readout of proximity to the missiles. Once you're within twenty feet, you'll know in which direction everything is."

"What if it's in the room above me?"

Alex shrugged. "There are no guarantees, but I'm sure you'll figure out a way of anything thrown at you. After all, you're Brady Hawk."

Hawk sighed. "And how am I supposed to get in without alerting the entire floor that I'm about to crash through a door?"

"Use this," Alex said, handing a card to Hawk. "I cloned the master key so you could get in."

"How did you—"

"Sleight of hand," she said with a wink. "Now get going. We don't have much time."

Hawk opened the door and entered the hallway. Activating the homing app on his phone, he waited for a moment for it to orient itself. Seconds later, the screen started flashing. A small box popped up at the bottom, directing Hawk where to go to discover the missiles. He needed to go up another floor.

Hawk eased his cart onto an elevator and selected

the highest floor in the hotel. But when he did, the button's light immediately went out as if he hadn't pushed it at all.

Moving his card in front of a security panel, Hawk heard a beep. He pushed the button for the twelfth floor again. This time, the elevator hummed to life and pulled Hawk up. When the doors slid open, he eased his cart into the hallway and followed the directions.

"Two doors down," Hawk said to Alex through his com device.

"Copy that."

Hawk knocked on the door. "Room service."

After waiting a few seconds and not hearing any movement inside, he waved his card in front of the access panel and unlocked the door. He wheeled the cart inside and was surprised to find a man there.

"*Lo siento*," Hawk said, apologizing in Spanish.

The man scowled and started speaking in Arabic. He waved his arms and moved aggressively toward Hawk. Picking up the lid to the tray, Hawk smashed the man in the face, stunning him. He staggered for a second and attempted to gain his bearings. Hawk charged the man, driving him backward and slamming his head into the wall. With two solid punches to the face, Hawk knocked out the man.

"Having fun yet?" Alex asked.

"Whoever this guy is, he looked stunned to see someone in his room."

Hawk took the man's gun and swept the rest of the suite. Just as Hawk was ready to declare the area clear, he entered the bathroom. Cowering in the corner, he found a half-naked woman clutching her bra across her chest.

Hawk motioned with his gun for her to leave. She jumped to her feet and scrambled out of the room, putting her clothes on hurriedly as she left.

"Now I know why he looked so surprised and angry," Hawk said.

"What'd you find?"

"He had a hooker in the room, but I let her leave."

"Did you find the missiles?"

"I found three of them here in the closet."

"And the fourth?"

"I'm still looking."

"Well, the GPS says it's there."

Hawk rummaged around the room, opening drawers and looking in closets for the other missile. After an exhaustive search, he finally found a case underneath the bed. He yanked it out into the middle of the room and opened the locks.

"Alex, we've got a problem."

"What is it?"

"Apparently, those tracking devices are embedded in the case, not the missiles. There's one missing."

"Damn you, Colton," she said.

"And I can assure you that it isn't here. We're going to have to widen our search."

Hawk used the cart's decorative black apron to hide the three missile cases as much as possible. On his way out the door, he noticed a laptop on a nearby desk. He stooped over to look at what was open on the web browser: an article from a news site about this evening's rally.

"We need to hurry," Hawk said. "Looks like they might intend on using that missile tonight."

"What did you see?"

"A laptop on the desk is open to a page about President Young's appearance at Hard Rock Stadium in Miami at a campaign rally with Oscar Fuentes."

"Hawk, when is that rally taking place?"

He skimmed the article and then glanced at his watch. "Less than two hours from now."

"Better hurry back. Whoever has these missiles is going after the president."

CHAPTER 20

BLUNT BUTTONED HIS SHIRT and tucked it into his pants. After tightening the belt, he turned and looked at himself in the mirror. It had been a long time since he'd put on a uniform of any kind, but this was a first for him—suiting up as a police officer.

He adjusted the badge on his shirt and took a deep breath. Impersonating a police officer was a crime, but that was rather benign on his list of illegal activity for the day. Blunt took his pledge to protect his country seriously, even if that meant breaking a few laws.

After having made bail for his earlier run in with the Union Station police, the officer in charge refused to return all of Blunt's belongings, claiming they were evidence a theft was committed. Blunt was given his keys and wallet, but nothing else. Yet there was only one other thing in his pocket besides the device he used to cut open the locker: the flash drive he'd found in the envelope. That small memory stick was also what likely got Lee Hendridge killed. Blunt needed to find out what was on it, laws be damned.

Blunt made the short drive to the precinct where he was processed and got out of his car. He walked up to the door, took a deep breath, and strode inside like he had been doing it every day of his adult life.

Dressed in uniform and wearing a cap along with a fake mustache, Blunt was barely recognizable from his arrest earlier that day. It also helped that no one who had processed him was still on the clock. A whole new shift oblivious to the arrest of a crazy old man breaking into Union Station lockers.

Blunt navigated through the station toward the back, following the signs to the evidence room in the basement. As he walked farther away from the offices and descended the stairs, the cacophony of officers talking on the phone or discussing arrest details with colleagues faded. The only sound Blunt could hear was the hum of the fluorescent lights overhead.

At the end of the hallway, a man was situated behind a counter, reading a newspaper. Approaching the man, Blunt tried to gauge what kind of fight he was in for. Was the guy a stickler for the rules or simply passing time? The answer to that question would determine how difficult it would be to gain access and take the flash drive back.

Blunt jammed his hand into his pants pocket and felt for the duplicate drive, the one he would replace in the evidence locker. To avoid drawing suspicion, Blunt had removed the most recent files, making sure that the ones remaining on the flash drive coincided with the time Lee Hendridge was alive.

Once Blunt reached the counter, he placed both hands on it and tapped out a little drumbeat in an attempt to get the man's attention. Instead of looking up, he kept his head down, apparently engrossed in the article.

"Excuse me," Blunt said, straining to read the officer's name on his badge.

The man still said nothing.

"Barker," Blunt said, "are you going to help me, or should I just go back there and get what I need by myself?"

Barker snapped out of his trance and looked at Blunt. "I'm sorry, Officer—" Barker said, staring at Blunt's nametag, "Officer Tyson."

"No worries," Blunt said. "I just need to get into the evidence locker for a minute and check something out."

Barker slid a clipboard across the counter toward Blunt. "Just fill this out, and then let me know when you're ready to proceed."

Blunt followed the directions and listed all the

pertinent information, including the case number, which he got off his arrest record. He returned the document, which Barker glanced at.

"Got your signature here," Barker mumbled to himself. "Looks like you're ready to go. Just make sure you wear gloves. And remember that you're on camera the whole time."

He reached under the counter and pressed a button. A buzzer sounded and a latch clicked, unlocking the chain link gate that led inside. Blunt glanced back at Barker, who had returned to reading his newspaper. Taking a minute to familiarize himself with the layout and the organizational structure of the room, Blunt navigated straight to the area where the evidence from his arrest had been filed.

Blunt slipped on a pair of gloves and opened the folder containing the envelope and flash drive. He retrieved the device, studying it for a moment before switching the two. After returning the file to its prescribed location, he headed to the locker exit. He cleared his throat, which got Barker's attention. Still engrossed in the paper, Barker buzzed the gate open without even looking up then slid the clipboard across the counter toward Blunt.

"Record your time out."

Blunt glanced at his watch and jotted down 6:45 p.m.

"Have a nice day," Barker said, his eyes still focused on the article he was reading.

Blunt walked back through the precinct, acknowledging a pair of friendly officers who nodded politely at him. When he reached his car, he climbed inside and let out a sigh of relief. He drove straight home and lumbered inside so he could immediately inspect the flash drive.

Drumming his fingers on the desk while the computer whirred to life, he looked at his phone to see he'd missed another call from Alex. He decided to call her as soon as he finished perusing the information Lee Hendridge had compiled.

Blunt opened the first file he saw, which was a large spreadsheet. He scrolled down a long list of names, many that he recognized. Next to each one was a brief description of their country affiliation followed by their duties and sphere of influence.

He then opened another document and started reading what appeared to be the introduction to Hendridge's big bombshell of a story. Blunt's mouth fell agape, and he promptly broke his promise. Instead of calling Alex back, he dialed Rebecca Paris's number.

"Ms. Paris, this is J.D. Blunt. I was able to retrieve a flash drive from the locker at Union Station. We need to talk."

CHAPTER 21

Varadero, Cuba

RETURNING THE MISSILES back to his hotel room, Hawk wasted no time in strategizing with Alex about the possible whereabouts of the fourth missile. With President Young scheduled to go on stage at the Oscar Fuentes rally in less than two hours, they needed to locate the missile before it was too late.

"Well, obviously we can't track this missile the way we did these others," Alex said. "But we know that missile was in that same hotel room."

"Are you thinking what I'm thinking?" Hawk said.

"I hope so."

Hawk winked. "How's your Spanish?"

* * *

TEN MINUTES LATER, Alex was dressed to the nines as she exited their room.

"You sure you can pull this off?" Hawk asked.

"If you get caught, you know the Cubans are going to throw us in prison."

"At least we'll be in prison together."

"I doubt that."

"A girl can dream, can't she," Alex said with a chuckle.

"Let's just make sure it doesn't end up that way."

Alex took the universal key card from Hawk and used it to access the basement floor on the elevator. Once there, she followed the signs to the security office.

Alex took the card and the lead. She unlocked the door and strode into a dark room where two men sat staring at a bank of video monitors.

One of the men spun around in his chair, eyebrows arched as he spoke.

"May I help you?" he asked in Spanish.

"I hope so," Alex responded in Spanish, her accent flawless. "I am Maria Olivar from the corporate offices of Telestar Systems. We're here to inspect your security system and make sure the equipment is working properly."

The man furrowed his brow. "I didn't receive any advance notice that you would be here," he said. "Just let me verify that with my supervisor."

"Don't go through all that trouble," Alex said. "I won't bother you more than a minute or two. It's just a routine checkup."

The man sighed. "Fine. What do you need to see?"

"I want to see if the cameras are functioning properly along with the playback features."

Alex scanned the labels on all the monitors until she identified the twelfth floor cameras. "Can you move the camera in the upper right corner onto the main screen?"

The man punched a few buttons on his keyboard, sending the feed onto a large screen.

"Run this footage back to four hours ago," she said.

The man obliged.

"Now fast forward," she said.

After a few seconds, a woman appeared on the screen, exiting the twelfth floor room. She was toting an odd-shaped piece of luggage along with a more traditional roller bag.

There it is.

Alex noted the woman looked somewhat familiar.

Glancing at the time stamp on the screen, she requested the man move the parking garage cameras to the main screen, splitting it into four, and backtrack to a couple of minutes after the woman had left her room.

"This doesn't seem like a routine checkup to me," one of the men said. "Most of the time, there are other diagnostics your company runs."

"We have multiple methods we employ while assessing our equipment's functionality," Alex snapped.

The woman was captured putting the two pieces of luggage into her trunk and leaving. She exited north out of the garage onto the main street.

She memorized the car's license plate number along with the make and model.

"You really need to upgrade to HD cameras," Alex said. "These images are still sufficient, but you won't be able to identify anyone definitively."

The man chuckled. "Most people come here so they won't be identified."

"I see," Alex said. "Well, thank you for your time."

As Alex turned to leave, the door opened, and a tall man wearing a bowler hat strode inside.

"What's going on here?" the stranger asked.

"I'm Maria Oliva from the Telestar Systems corporate offices, and I'm just leaving," Alex said.

"No, you're not," the man said.

"Excuse me," she said, trying to slide past him. "I must be going."

He shifted over, blocking her path. "You're not going anywhere until I figure out who you are."

"I already told you that I'm—"

The man glared at her. "Stop lying."

"I'm not lying. I'm—"

"You're not with Telestar, because I am."

Alex's eyes widened as the man whipped out a gun and trained it on her. "You're coming with me," he said with a growl. "We're going to straighten this out elsewhere."

CHAPTER 22

Hard Rock Stadium
Miami, Florida

SENATOR THURMAN WALTZED out onto the stage covering the area that was the end zone during Miami Dolphins games. A thunderous applause erupted as the song "Country Must be Country Wide" blared on the loudspeakers. His longtime relationship with President Young resulted in an invitation to introduce him at the Oscar Fuentes rally. With the country's seemingly unstable political situation, including the recent death of the former president, voters were registering all over the place in polls when asked their preference for which party should be running the country. And no incumbent was going to leave anything to chance.

Thurman was grateful he wasn't up for re-election for another four years, but he was happy to help his fellow state senator hang on to his seat. Even if Young hadn't asked Thurman to participate, he probably would've done it anyway. He and Fuentes weren't the best of friends, but they held similar values when it came to voting records on Capitol Hill.

With a megawatt smile, Thurman waved and waited for the applause to die down. He put his hands up to quiet the crowd before he began.

"Tonight I have the privilege of getting to introduce to you one of the finest men our country has ever had in the White House. He's the right man at the right time. And I couldn't be prouder to serve under him as a member of Congress."

Thurman had grown accustomed to lying. The more he did it, the easier it became. Five years ago, his statement would've been completely true. But it wasn't any more. Thurman and Young had done more than drift apart—they'd almost become adversarial. However, no one would've known it judging from their warm embrace on stage as Thurman welcomed Young to speak.

Like most rising stars in the senate, Thurman made his presidential ambitions public. As a former Marine, author of dozens of high-profile bills, and member of esteemed senate committees, he checked all the political boxes when it came to the kind of candidate both parties wanted to put forth in a general election. Then there was the matter of Thurman's rugged good looks and charming personality. In one sense, he was almost too good to be true. But there were some downsides.

Two nasty and very public divorces along with a scuffle on the senate floor in which he decked a representative from the opposing party that made Thurman radioactive. But Young never stood up for Thurman when he was being assaulted by the press. However, the big blow came when Young reneged on his promise to appoint Thurman as the secretary of state. Thurman had seen that position as the final feather in his proverbial political cap. He would have experience in diplomacy as well as legislation, giving him the broad perspective he needed to govern more effectively. At least, that's how the pundits would've seen it. But a broken pledge led to a severed relationship. Publicly, the two men still appeared to be in each other's good graces. But that was only because such a move was politically expedient for both of them. A fractured party was the last thing either of them wanted, even more so than cutting ties with a former friend who was either viewed as a liability or a backstabber.

Thurman had wisely kept the slight to himself, but he hadn't forgotten.

While Young droned on about how the nation could come together and experience a much-needed healing of divisions under the leadership of someone like Fuentes, Thurman slipped off to a quiet corner backstage to make a phone call.

"How are things going?" Thurman asked.

"They're going fine at the moment," the man on the other line said. "I tracked them down and captured the woman. They flew to Cuba just like you suspected."

"And the man?"

"He's still on the lam."

"You better be careful," Thurman said. "He's dangerous."

"Don't worry. I'm going to use her as bait. They won't interfere with your other plans for this evening; that much I'm sure of."

"Good. Keep me posted."

Thurman hung up and rushed toward his three staffers. He furrowed his brow as he approached them.

"What is it?" one of the women asked.

"Is everything okay?" another inquired.

Thurman nodded subtly. "I need to get out of here right now."

"What's going on?" another staffer asked.

"They found the man who murdered my son," Thurman said. "I need to get back to our hotel so I can get fully briefed."

"Absolutely," one of the staffers said. "I'll run and get your stuff right now."

"Thank you," Thurman said. "I appreciate it. Just please move as quickly as you can. I'm anxious to find out the full extent of what happened and who the scumbag is who did this to Thaxton."

"Of course, sir," one of the staffers said.

Less than two minutes later, Thurman was in an SUV, wearing a faint smile as the car sped away from the stadium.

CHAPTER 23

BLUNT STOOD AT THE BACK entrance to The Phoenix Foundation and waited for Rebecca Paris to arrive. Even though it was well after regular business hours, he didn't want to risk any stragglers see her enter the building.

When she arrived at the door, Blunt pushed it open and waved her inside.

"We're going to go up the back stairwell," he said. "Hope you don't mind."

Paris shook her head. "Fine with me."

She was wearing a black knee-length skirt with a white blouse and three-inch heels. Blunt noted how she was almost eye-level with him.

"What's going on?" she asked as they trudged up the steps.

"Let's wait until we get upstairs before we discuss this any further." Blunt led her inside his team's suite and escorted her to his office. "Please, have a seat," he said, gesturing to the chair across from his desk.

She eased into the chair and crossed her legs.

"You have me really curious now," Rebecca said, leaning forward.

Blunt leaned back in his chair, interlocking his fingers and placing them behind his head. "Everything I'm about to show you and tell you about his highly classified, but I trust that you won't print or share anything you see here today. Can I have your word on that?"

She nodded. "So what exactly did Lee stumble upon?"

"What I found—he didn't stumble onto it. The information on the flash drive that I took from the locker had to be gleaned from an in-depth investigation, perhaps over several years."

"Can I take a look at it myself?" she asked.

"Sure," Blunt said. He jammed the flash drive into his laptop and hammered on the keyboard. He opened up a few files and spun the computer around so she could see it.

"What am I looking at?" she asked.

"It's a list of names and affiliations from key leaders, influential business people, and military personnel from around the world."

She scrolled down the screen and furrowed her

brow. "This is bizarre. What's the connection between all these people?"

"Take a look at one of the other files I opened on there for you. It's a written document, which appears to be the introduction to his big expose—and the knowledge of which ultimately got him killed."

Rebecca spent a few minutes in silence perusing the words of her late boyfriend. Blunt could only imagine how haunting they would be for her. When she finished, she looked up with wide eyes.

"You've been around Washington a long time and involved with military types," she said. "What do you make of all this? Had Lee gone insane? I've never heard of such an organization."

Blunt sighed and crossed his arms. "I've been really hesitant to poke around on this right now," he said. "Lee called this group Obsidian, which sounds like something straight out of a conspiracy website. A global shadow agency that conspires to control everything with designs on creating a one world order. If that isn't the greatest fear of all conspiracy hounds, I don't know what is."

"But in the article, Lee suggested that Obsidian is doing more than just controlling governments and countries—they're squashing and absorbing the ones who don't comply."

"I was afraid to even type the word *obsidian* into

the search engine on my computer, but I did attempt to verify some of his claims and cross-reference them with the list of names provided on the spreadsheet."

"And?" Rebecca asked, her eyes widening.

"They seem to check out. Just do a search for all the individuals the UN currently has sanctions against. There are several key UN ambassadors on the list, and they played varying roles in pushing these sanctions through. All they would have to do is drum up some false charges, verify it with UN inspectors who are in Obsidian's back pocket, and *voila*—crippling sanctions."

"These people are everywhere," she said, scrolling back through the list.

Blunt nodded. "That's what I found most fascinating. The UN ties are just the tip of the iceberg. I found leaders from Russia, Germany, England, Australia, China, Italy, and France among others. It's such a vast network that I'm not sure how you could go about dismantling it. Hell, there are even reporters and editors at prominent news organizations in on this, if Lee's research is all spot on. And I have no reason to think he isn't, especially since it's what led to his demise."

"Let me write about it," Rebecca said. "I could do it anonymously through The Skinny's website."

Blunt shook his head. "Absolutely not. If these

people are half as powerful as we think they are, they'll figure out that you're behind it within an hour of it getting posted online. They'll kill the story and likely you along with it."

"Once it's public, they couldn't do anything to me. Murdering me would just be a tacit admission of guilt. They would be completely exposed and would have far too many tracks to cover if we released all this information."

Blunt sighed. "I promise you that this would be dismissed as the ramblings of a crazy man. And if you survived—and that's a big if—you would immediately be branded as a wacko and alienated from your entire profession. Once you escaped the limelight, someone from Obsidian would take you out. Look, this stuff frightens me, but you can't just go charging up a network so well connected and funded without a systematic way to take them apart and eliminate all the players."

"So I'm supposed to just sit around and do nothing?" she asked.

"No, I don't want you to sit around," Blunt said. "I want you to start building dossiers on each one of these people. Investigate the individuals, not the entire organization. If we have a well-sourced report about what these individuals are up to, both on their own and as part of Obsidian, we could begin to go after them."

"*We?*"

"Yes, us—The Phoenix Foundation."

"What exactly do you do here?"

"Let's not talk about that right now," Blunt said. "It's not really relevant to this conversation. Just know that I have a team who operates internationally and can address situations like this. I'm just telling you for your own peace of mind that this isn't going to just sit on my desk. We're going to look into this and verify its veracity—and see what we can do about it."

"I'll refrain from publishing anything about this, but can you still get me a copy of the flash drive?"

"What for?" Blunt asked. "This information is what got your boyfriend killed."

"I just want a copy of it for insurance, you know, just in case I get threatened."

"I'm not sure it's the wisest idea," Blunt said. "If they know you have all this information, they just might murder you right there."

"Can you do me this one favor please?"

"Okay, fine," Blunt said, reaching into his desk and producing a flash drive. "I made a backup for myself, but take it. Just, please, don't ever let it see the light of day, for your own sake."

She smiled. "I appreciate your help, Mr. Blunt. You know, what people say about you around the Capitol isn't true. You are a sincere man who believes passionately in what you do."

Blunt chuckled. "I wouldn't believe everything you hear."

Rebecca stood and headed toward the door. She grabbed the doorknob and stopped. "I've got one more question."

"Fire away."

"I didn't see a chain of command on that spreadsheet. Is there someone in charge of Obsidian?"

Blunt swallowed hard and shook his head. "I didn't see anything in those documents that suggested who it might be."

"Okay. Thanks. I really do appreciate all you did to get this for me."

Blunt walked her downstairs, opening the door to let her out the back exit. Once she was out of sight, Blunt leaned against the wall and closed his eyes. He hoped she couldn't tell he was lying.

CHAPTER 24

Varadero, Cuba

SAMUEL GETTY WENT by the codename Elias, a tip he picked up by watching Brazilian soccer. Make it easy and memorable. The name Elias sounded far more menacing than Sam or Mr. Getty. He also learned that whenever Senator Thurman called with an "opportunity," Elias would be a fool to turn it down.

He jammed his gun into the back of the woman he'd found posing as a security systems expert from a corporate office. She went by the name of Alex, but he didn't care. She was just another job to him, another person someone wanted dead. However, her kill fee was paltry compared to her partner, Brady Hawk. That's why Elias was going to use her as bait.

"Who are you?" Alex asked, resisting his shoves down the stairs.

"Just shut up and keep walking," he said.

"I'm not going another step until you tell me who you are."

"Fine," Elias said. "I'll just carry you myself."

She spun around and looked him in the eyes, but Elias made sure it was the last thing she saw before pistol whipping her in the head. He collected her body after she collapsed and then hustled through the door and across the dimly lit parking garage. After he unlocked the door, he tossed her unconscious body into the back seat and cranked up the car.

Once he settled behind the steering wheel, he looked over his shoulder once more to check and make sure she was still out. Satisfied, he grinned and reached to put the car into gear when a bullet ripped through the window and the back of his head.

Elias fell face first onto the steering wheel, landing on the horn. It blared, echoing throughout the parking garage.

* * *

HAWK HUSTLED OVER to the car and yanked a dead body out of the driver's seat. He ripped the man's coat off and used it to clean the windshield so he could see while driving. After tossing the coat on top of the man, Hawk opened the door to the backseat where Alex was starting to come to.

"Hey, Alex, it's me. Are you okay?"

With her eyes still closed, she grimaced and then

touched her temples. "What just happened?"

"The man who captured you in the security room is dead, and you're safe."

"What did I miss?" she asked.

"Hold that thought."

Hawk raced across the parking garage and grabbed the luggage cart with the three missiles on it. He pushed it back toward the abductor's car and loaded the missiles into the trunk along with all their gear—except for Alex's computer.

"I need you to wake up," he said.

"My head," she said as she groaned. "It hurts."

"Drink this," Hawk said, handing her a bottle.

She took it and chugged all the water.

"What's happening?" she asked after finishing.

"We're not out of the woods yet. There's still one more missile out there, and we need to go find it."

"Do you know where to look?" Alex asked.

"I was hoping you could help with that."

Alex moaned. "Let me think for a second. I saw the car that drove away with the missile. A woman was driving. She looked familiar."

"You recognized her?" Hawk asked.

"I thought so, but the resolution on the monitors wasn't that sharp."

"What else do you remember?"

"Just give me a second. It's coming back to me—

the license plate. And she left in a blue sedan, heading north onto the main road."

Hawk thrust the computer into her lap. "Try to remember as many details as you can, but we have to find that missile before they launch it toward Miami."

Hawk jammed the gear into reverse and backed out of the space. Seconds later, he was screeching his tires as he sped out of the garage and onto the main road. As Hawk drove, Alex typed furiously on her laptop.

"Making any progress?" he asked after about a minute.

"I'm accessing some CIA satellites, but there aren't that many cars in the area. It shouldn't be too difficult to find."

Hawk sped along the road, contemplating how he would handle the terrorists with just a handgun. It wasn't a scenario that set him up for success, but at least he had a weapon. That was a far better improvement than his situation an hour earlier when he didn't even have the other three missiles, much less a gun.

"Okay, I think I found the car," Alex said. "Up ahead on the left, there's a short road that leads to an inlet. It's hard to tell because it's dark, but I'm pretty sure that's the car."

"If you're wrong about this, Alex—"

"I'm sure this is it," she said. "Just turn left up here."

Hawk followed her directions, whipping the car onto the tight two-lane road. It wound around for several hundred yards before Alex told him to kill the lights.

"Better hurry," Alex said. "I've got a live feed, and it looks like someone is loading up a rocket launcher of some sort."

"How far away are we?" Hawk asked.

"Maybe fifty yards around the bend," she said.

"If they're arming the weapon, I'll never make it in time."

"But they might hear you," Alex protested.

"We don't have a chance now unless we do."

Hawk eased his car around the curve, creeping slowly. The moon illuminated the beach in front of them. A woman and three men were all crouched over some object, working feverishly.

"That's got to be the launcher," Hawk said. "I'm getting out."

Hawk hustled toward the beach but stopped short when he saw one of the men hoist the weapon onto his shoulder and fire the missile. Flames streaked out the back as it tore through the sky. The terrorists all threw their hands in the air and celebrated, shouting something in Arabic.

That's Evana Bahar.

"Get back here," Alex said over the coms.

"No," Hawk said. "We need to take them out."

"What we need to do is get the hell outta here and call Miami right now to get them to clear the stadium. We only have about fifteen minutes before the missile hits."

"That's not enough time," Hawk said. "They'll never be able to clear the area in time."

"We've got to try," Alex said.

Hawk turned and raced back toward the car—but not before one of the men spotted him.

Several bullets peppered the ground nearby as Hawk continued his sprint. The car was already running thanks to Alex. As soon as Hawk reached the car, another bullet pinged the side door, followed by one more that hit the windshield.

Hawk jumped into the driver's seat and stomped on the gas. One more bullet tore through the back windshield, shattering the glass.

"Go, go, go!" Alex screamed frantically.

In the rearview mirror, Hawk watched a set of headlights flicker on. The terrorists' vehicle roared after them.

CHAPTER 25

Washington, D.C.

MALLORY KAUFFMAN SLIPPED her key into the lock and opened the door to her ground floor apartment. While her work at the NSA might have been exciting, her return home each night was devoid of fanfare and rather depressing. Most nights, the most exciting event was when her cat, Bugsy, greeted her by rubbing up against her leg. Bugsy would purr for a moment and then demand food.

But after a few seconds of being inside, Mallory could tell something was off. Bugsy was nowhere to be found, and she suddenly had a bad vibe. Mallory's hand trembled as she reached for the light switch on the far wall. She flipped the lamp on and hoped to discover that nothing was wrong.

Instead of finding her home like she'd left it, Mallory stared at the contents of her living room sprawled out in front of her. The couch cushions were scattered all over. The coffee table was splintered and lying on its side. On the far wall, a pair of Monet prints she had on canvas had been slashed.

Mallory rushed into the kitchen and grabbed her gun from the back of her utensil drawer. Extending her arms, she trained the gun on the area in front of her and moved slowly through the house. Tears streamed down her face, a mix of terror and anger. She used her sleeve to wipe them away as she walked.

Her bedroom was the worst of all. Mallory narrowed her eyes and stared at her bed, the mattress shredded. Stuffing poured out of rips and tears created by a blade. All of her clothes were strewn across the floor. And the thing that made her most upset was her journal on her bed stand, open to a page in the center. The violation of everything both private and sacred to her was almost too much to bear.

Sobbing wildly, Mallory leaned against the wall and slid to the floor. A robbery was one thing, but this appeared to be malicious, almost vengeful. If only she could explain it away by blaming it on an ex-boyfriend. But there was nothing that made sense in the moment.

Mallory didn't move for the next five minutes. She called for Bugsy several times, but her cat didn't come. That's when Mallory decided to get up and go look for her. Still toting the gun, Mallory eased through the rest of the apartment.

"Bugsy," she said, trying to steady her voice. "Where are you? I know you're hungry. Where are you, girl?"

Still nothing.

Mallory went into the guest room where Bugsy often liked to hide. "Bugsy, stop playing around. I know you might be scared, but Mama's home now."

Mallory knelt to look under the bed. She smiled when she saw her cat, back arched, all the way against the wall.

"They're gone now," Mallory said. "It's okay, Bugsy. You can come out now."

Bugsy crept over toward Mallory before leaping into her arms. The cat purred excitedly.

"It's all right, girl. I've got you now."

Mallory held Bugsy tight, nuzzling her face against the cat's head. But Bugsy continued to act nervous.

"What is it?" Mallory asked. "It's just me here."

With her eyes closed and still snuggling with the cat, Mallory turned around and then opened her eyes. She shrieked at what she saw, scaring Bugsy, who bounded away and landed on the bed.

On the near wall was a giant symbol in red spray paint.

"Did you see the people who did this, Bugsy?" Mallory asked.

Mallory set her gun down and then fished her camera out of her pocket. She snapped several pictures of the image and texted it to Alex. If anyone would know what the mark meant, Alex would.

After a couple minutes without a reply from Alex, Mallory called.

Following one ring, the call went straight to Alex's voicemail.

"Dammit, Alex. Pick up the phone."

Mallory called again. Still no response.

She collapsed on the bed next to Bugsy, who walked tentatively up to Mallory before lying down on her chest.

"I don't know whoever did this, but they're not going to intimidate me," Mallory said, stroking her cat. "We'll get through this."

Bugsy darted off Mallory's chest and dove onto the floor in a sudden flash. Mallory just thought the cat had returned to being her playful self. A second later, a bullet crashed through the window, followed by several more shots.

Mallory followed Bugsy's lead, diving onto the floor. More bullets tore through the window, peppering the far wall.

Hunched over in a fetal position, Mallory covered her head. She pulled Bugsy close to her and prayed for the shooting to stop.

CHAPTER 26

Varadero, Cuba

SITUATED ON A THIN PENINSULA forming the boundary of the Bay of Cárdenas, Varadero kept things simple. The resort town consisted of one long road with beachfront property on both sides. As a place to visit and relax, Varadero was heaven. But when it came to finding a place to hide from raging terrorists, the small city was hell.

Hawk tightened his grip on the steering wheel and checked his rearview mirror. Less than a hundred meters behind him, the blue sedan roared in pursuit.

"There's a turnoff up ahead on the right," Alex said, pointing in the distance.

Darkness had fallen on the island, and Hawk wasn't familiar with the road to identify a safe place to take cover. But it certainly wasn't going to happen with the terrorists still on his tail.

"They're too close," Hawk said. "They'll follow

us, and then what? We don't know if that's a dead end or not. The last thing I want right now is to get back into a corner with them."

"Okay, I'm just trying to help."

"You've got bigger problems right now that require your attention. You need to hack into the navigational system on that missile and splash it down into the Atlantic."

"I'm working on it," Alex said, her head down as she typed on her laptop.

"Can you do it?" he asked.

"Keep your fingers crossed. I got the specs from Colton Industries earlier, so I got everything I need to do it. I'm just not sure I have enough time."

"Just focus on that," Hawk said. "You've got less than two minutes. I'll figure out how to shake these thugs."

Hawk stomped on the gas as he approached a slight curve. He was getting close to the center of town where he would be more vulnerable not only to the terrorists but also to local police. If caught by either one, Hawk knew the chances of them escaping with their lives would be small. There was no extraction team waiting for them either. Hawk had to figure out a way.

Fight or die.

"Hold on," Hawk said.

He whipped the steering wheel to his left just as he rounded the slight curve. If his tail lights vanished from view, he thought he might be able to trick the terrorists just enough to race back down the street and steal down a side road and wait them out.

Rerouted in the opposite direction, Hawk smiled as he thought his plan had worked. The terrorists flew right past. But the victory was short-lived as he looked in his rearview mirror and noticed the blue sedan turning around.

"Dammit," he said.

"Going that well?" Alex asked without looking up, her fingers flying across the laptop.

"I hope things are going better for you."

"I'm getting there, just running out of time."

Hawk checked his mirrors. The blue sedan might have followed him, but his earlier maneuver would have given him the separation he needed to escape them for good. With his foot all the way to the floorboard, he gave Alex another warning.

"Brace yourself," he said.

For a fleeting second, the blue sedan's headlights vanished in the distance—and Hawk seized his chance. He spun the car around again in the opposite direction, wasting no time in jamming his foot back onto the gas pedal. The car lurched forward, thrusting Hawk and Alex back in their seats.

"You sure know how to show a girl a good time," Alex said, her head still buried in her computer.

"Have you managed to take control of that missile yet?" he asked as they raced past the blue sedan.

"I'm almost there."

"Better hurry. We've only got—"

"Thirty seconds. Trust me, I know."

Hawk glanced in his rearview mirror. He slammed his fist on the dashboard as he noticed that he hadn't managed to fool the terrorists. They turned sharply and were once again in pursuit. While he was still miffed at his inability to shake the car, his disappointment was abated by Alex's announcement.

"I'm in," she said triumphantly.

"You've got ten seconds."

"That's more than enough," she said, her fingers a blur across the keyboard.

She hit a button emphatically and pumped her fist. "Done," she said. "Take that!"

"Where'd you put the missile down?" Hawk asked.

"It's going to land about twenty miles off shore, far away from any humans. And I think the chemicals may get diluted in the salt water, but the bottom line is nobody is going to die tonight."

Hawk looked in his mirror and shook his head. "I wouldn't make that declaration just yet."

Alex turned around and let a string of curse words fly. "Got any new ideas?" she asked. "Seems like this U-turn plan isn't working."

Hawk glanced behind him as he saw the headlights disappear. Seconds later, all he saw were red tail lights. "What the hell?"

Alex looked over his shoulder. "What is it?"

"They just turned around."

"Well, that's good, isn't it?"

"Yeah, but it doesn't make—" Hawk stopped short and slowed the car as he noticed a police roadblock a quarter of a mile down the road. If that wasn't disconcerting enough, a helicopter flew directly over them.

"It makes perfect sense now," Alex said. "So, now what?"

"Well, we can't let those cops stop us. I think we should turn around, see if we can find out what group was behind this attack."

"Sounds like a suicide mission," Alex said. "I thought you were into the whole live-to-fight-another-day school of thought?"

"Didn't you say that woman was carrying two large suitcases out of the hotel?"

Alex nodded. "What are you thinking?"

"What if the other suitcase contained another weapon?"

"We got all four missiles that Colton told us about. You think he omitted something?"

"I doubt it, but what if the other suitcase was the Silencer 2K? What if Thurman gave this to the terrorists as well? We can't let them have technology like that. They'd be able to sneak around and wreak havoc all over the place without being seen. It'd make them next to impossible to catch."

"So, what do you propose we do about it?"

"Let's go track them down."

Hawk slowly turned around before gunning the engine. He didn't go more than a hundred meters before the police cars abandoned their roadblock and began pursuit.

"We've got company now," Hawk said.

"We can handle them later, but we can't let those terrorists get a chance to utilize that technology. It'll be disastrous."

"Just be ready to drive," Hawk said.

"You have a plan?"

"Still working on it. But I'll go after the terrorists; you're going to have to shake these cops. We're already going to be in trouble with the Cubans for our actions here, but if they discover these weapons in our trunk, we'll never see the light of day again."

"Teamwork makes the dream work," Alex said.

"Somehow I've got a feeling that you didn't mean

that sincerely."

"Actually, this is exactly what I imagined our marriage to be like—and I wouldn't want it any other way."

"No relaxing on the beach and sipping margaritas?"

"Maybe once or twice a year, but that'd get boring fast."

Hawk chuckled. "Speaking of fast, we're going to have to make this switch quickly for you to have a chance. We're coming up on the beach."

A few hundred meters ahead, Hawk watched the helicopter touch down on the sand, swirling it around. His headlights cut through the darkness, illuminating the scene. The mystery woman handed a suitcase to one of the guards and hustled toward the chopper. They pulled her aboard as the military-style aircraft didn't have doors.

Hawk got as close as he could and slammed on the brakes. "It's all you now," he said. "Drive like hell. Good luck."

"You, too," Alex said.

Hawk bolted out of the car and sprinted toward the helicopter. As he neared the aircraft, he shielded his eyes from the sand whipping through the air. The helicopter's engine whined as the rotor speed increased, signaling the pilot was preparing to take off.

Hawk put his head down and kept moving. Just

as he got within a few meters, the helicopter lifted off the ground. Hawk took a couple more steps before leaping and grabbing hold of one of the skids. Locking his arms around it, he swung back and forth, and the chopper pitched and yawed as it gained elevation.

He looked below and saw Alex speeding away with two police cars following her.

What have we gotten ourselves into?

CHAPTER 27

Miami, Florida

SENATOR THURMAN PACED around the luxury condominium atop the Four Seasons Hotel he had rented for the week. With constituents to visit in Florida, he couldn't resist booking a few days at the building that towered over Miami. He also thought it would be a great location to base his operations out of once the missile struck Hard Rock Stadium. It'd be his opportunity to be on the ground, posing for photos while helping with the recovery effort.

With the rally being televised live on several local channels, Thurman tuned in to watch the event unfold. But he was disappointed when nothing of consequence happened. No missiles. No explosions. No mass panic in the streets as people ran for their lives. Just President Young waving to people as he strolled off the stage.

Thurman picked up his burner phone and dialed

a number belonging to his contact in Cuba, Evana Bahar.

"What the hell just happened down there? I thought all systems were go."

"Apparently your assassin didn't do his job," Bahar said. "I can't be expected to thwart off one of the most deadly assassins in the world while trying to launch missiles into the middle of a political rally. Do you know how stressful that is?"

"Do you know what lengths I went to in order to make sure that the missile strike was a success?"

"Obviously, you didn't go far enough."

"Where are you now?"

"I'm on a helicopter, and Brady Hawk is trying to get on board."

"You'll never have a better chance to kill him than right now. I recommend you shoot him immediately."

"I would if I could, but our pilot is trying to shake him loose."

Thurman seethed as he paced around the apartment during the call. "If he climbs aboard, he'll kill you all."

Bahar chuckled. "Just be honest and tell me you don't care about us. You only care about your precious Silencer 2K. You realize this device is what's going to get you killed, don't you? They're going to be able to track everything back to you if you have it. Trust me—you don't really want this thing."

"At this point, I don't care what you do with it. Just make sure Brady Hawk is dead."

"Will you pay us in full if we do?"

"I'll pay you double if I get evidence of his dead body."

"That shouldn't be a problem."

"Great," Thurman said. "I'll look forward to your call."

He hung up and then slid his phone across the table. Collapsing into the couch, Thurman rolled up his sleeves before exhaling a long breath in frustration.

All he could do now was wait for Bahar's call.

* * *

ELANA BAHAR TIGHTENED her harness and checked her gun to make sure it was loaded. Flying above the Bay of Cárdenas, the helicopter swayed back and forth in an attempt to shake Hawk. Bahar decided she'd had enough, recognizing that such perpetual motion increased the difficulty of delivering a kill shot on Hawk, even if she was only a few meters away.

"Keep it steady," Bahar said into her headset's mic.

"We can't let him get aboard."

"And I'm not going to let him, but I need you to keep it steady so I can get him off the skids."

"I can't do that," he said, continuing to fling Hawk around with a constant dose of pitching and yawing.

"If you don't, the first bullet from my gun will be for you. Now increase the altitude and steady the chopper."

The pilot ignored her commands.

Bahar fired a shot into the cockpit, putting a hole in the front glass between the pilot and co-pilot. Both men slowly turned and glared at her.

"You were lucky that time," she said. "The next two shots I take will be into the back of your necks— and I'll take over. Have I made myself clear?"

"Understood," the pilot said. However, he failed to comply.

Despite her ability to fly a helicopter, she resisted the urge to shoot, recognizing that it would be nearly impossible to both pilot and fend off Hawk. She decided to take a different tact and appeal to their greed.

"Our client has agreed to double our fee if we can confirm the death of this man. Whatever you're doing isn't working as he's still clinging to the skids. Now take this chopper up before I take you out."

The pilot finally pulled back on the stick. The helicopter began to ascend, evening its keel as it rose.

She sighed, thankful that she didn't have to apply more pressure.

At least I know these two men are only in this for the money.

Bahar checked her harness one final time. Satisfied that she was ready to take her shot, she leaned outside, craning her neck to attain Hawk's location beneath the aircraft.

But when she peered over the edge, Hawk was nowhere to be seen.

"I think you lost him," Bahar said.

The pilot let out a celebratory whoop and high-fived his co-pilot before starting his descent.

Bahar couldn't see the other skid and wasn't ready to proclaim Hawk vanquished.

"Amir, what can you see on your side?" she asked the man who was sitting kitty-corner behind her.

He didn't answer.

"Amir?"

She turned and glanced over his shoulder.

Amir was gone.

CHAPTER 28

Varadero, Cuba

ALEX'S GAZE BOUNCED between the road and her rearview mirror, not that seeing if the police cars were still behind her was really necessary. The flashing lights made it obvious the cops weren't about to abandon their pursuit. Racing inland was the smart move, but it still didn't solve her ultimate problem of how to shake the officers. If she got caught now, the chances of escaping a Cuban prison sentence were next to nothing, never mind the fact that she had three short-range missiles in her trunk that contained lethal chemical agents.

Maybe I would prefer a life on the beach somewhere.

Alex considered all of her options. Outrunning the police seemed like the best option, but it also might sound the death knell for her escape plan should more police get summoned to assist in apprehending her. There was also the get out and make a run for it. The problem with that plan meant she and Hawk lost any mode of transportation and would complicate their exit from Cuba, something they needed to do immediately. She also could just surrender and beg for mercy. However, the stories of U.S. spies who'd been incarcerated by the Cubans were legendary. That would be a roll of the dice she wasn't willing to take. Declining all three of those options meant only one remained: deception.

Here goes nothing.

Alex swung a hard left onto the street leading up to the Varadero Azul Hotel. She headed straight for the fifth floor of the parking deck. In the distance, she could hear the screeching tires from the police cars still trailing her. However, she'd managed to gain a significant lead of two floors. She parked and took a deep breath before gathering her belongings and exiting the vehicle.

When the police cars roared around the corner, the officers barely looked at her. But when they noticed the vehicle they'd been chasing was parked and empty, they both threw their gears into reverse and backed up, blocking Alex's path to the stairwell.

Nonplussed by their movement, she moved nimbly around their vehicles and kept walking.

The officers scrambled out of their cars and ordered her to stop.

Alex complied. She turned slowly toward them.

"Is there a problem?" she asked in Spanish.

"What is your name?"

"My name is Maria Olivar," she said. "I'm making a service call for the hotel's security system."

The officers sauntered up to her.

"Let me see some identification," one of the men said.

"I'm sorry, but I'm in a hurry and must decline."

"I wasn't asking."

"*Buenas noches*," she said before spinning around and resuming her path toward the stairs.

"Do not walk away from us," the other officer said.

Alex froze and kept her back to the men. She raised her hands in the air.

"I don't know who you think I am, but you've got the wrong woman. Now, if you'll excuse me, my services are required immediately. And if I don't show up within an hour, we have to provide free repair service. My employer won't like that, especially if it happens on your account."

"What's in your hand?" one officer asked.

Alex clutched her key fob so hard she thought she might break it. But she refused to reveal the contents.

"I'll ask you one more time—what's in your

hand?"

Thinking quickly, Alex opened her hand, dropping the fob onto the ground. One of the officers knelt down to pick it up. When he did, Alex seized her opportunity. She whipped her computer bag off her shoulder and clocked the standing officer in the face. As the other officer scrambled to his feet, Alex turned and stomped on his knee. Doubling over in pain, he tried to keep his balance before Alex kicked him in head, knocking him out. The other officer who'd been stunned by the blow from Alex's bag staggered backward before regaining his balance. He then reached for his weapon. Alex slid to the ground and swept the officer's legs out from underneath him, resulting in a hard landing on his back. He groaned as he rolled over and tried to reach his gun. When he did, he noticed it wasn't there.

"Gotcha," Alex said before pistol whipping the officer.

He collapsed to the ground, unconscious.

Alex took one of the officer's keys and unlocked the trunk. She handcuffed both men and lugged them up and into the back of one of the cars. Before she left, she parked both cars, moving the one with the officers up to the top level, which was completely vacant.

Alex hustled back down a level to her car and

headed north along the main highway extending to the end of the peninsula and the Bay of Cárdenas. As she drove, she scanned the horizon for any sign of the helicopter. Worried that she'd lost Hawk, she eventually saw a chopper peeling back toward the bay.

It was too dark to tell what was happening, but she was determined to get a closer look.

CHAPTER 29

AS THE HELICOPTER LEVELED off, Hawk pulled himself up and peeked inside. He had a clear view of the back two rows with easy access to them both. His presence didn't go unnoticed as the man in the back saw Hawk and rushed toward him.

Clinging to the skid with his right arm, Hawk reached up and grabbed the man by the front of his shirt. Hawk was surprised how easily he moved the man. Based on his size, Hawk figured the guy couldn't have weighed more than a hundred and forty pounds soaking wet. Without getting much of a fight, Hawk ripped the man out of the helicopter, flinging him into the water below.

Hawk inched along the skid to get a better view of the three remaining passengers. Evana Bahar appeared upset, yelling at the pilots. A few seconds later, she fired a shot at the windshield.

This woman is insane.

He eased back along the skid, out of her line of sight.

A few moments later, he listened as she started calling out for the passenger Hawk had flung into the water.

"Amir, what can you see on your side?" Bahar asked.

No answer.

"Amir?" she asked.

At eye level with the floor, Hawk watched as Bahar craned her neck in search of Amir.

"Turn around," Bahar said to the pilot.

"What for? We need to get out of here."

"Turn around now," Bahar said. "Amir must have fallen out of the helicopter while you were trying to get rid of the American."

"We need to get out of here as soon as possible. The senator chartered a plane for us in the Florida Keys that will leave us if we aren't there on time."

"I'm not going back without Amir. We at least owe it to him to search the water."

The pilot banked hard to the right, turning around and heading back toward the Bay of Cárdenas. He descended until he was only about twenty meters above the water.

Hawk shimmied along the skid and scanned the cargo section of the chopper. Fastened to the back wall with a net were several large boxes. However, the carrying case for the Silencer 2K was easily identifiable with the Colton Industries logo emblazoned on the side.

The helicopter was getting close enough to the bay that the blades were whipping the salt water up into the air. With the mist hampering Hawk's grip and vision, he realized he didn't have much of a choice but to get onboard and attempt to seize control of the aircraft. He hoisted himself up and scrambled inside, surprising Bahar.

Her eyes widened as soon as she recognized Hawk. A shrill scream startled the pilots, who both turned around to see what was happening. Bahar fumbled for her gun, but Hawk was one step ahead of her. He lunged toward her, swatting the weapon out of her hands. Steadying herself by grabbing onto a handle near the doorway, she kicked Hawk in the chest. He staggered back against the far wall.

As Hawk got up, he reached inside the net and snatched the case handle for the Silencer 2K.

"No," Bahar said, scrambling around the seat to get to him.

Hawk swung the case toward her. She leaned back to avoid suffering a blow before going on the offensive. Rushing toward Hawk, she dove low in an effort to knock him off balance. But Hawk was ready for her, darting out of her path and allowing her to careen into the cargo hold.

Wasting no time, Hawk flung the case into the water.

"You bastard," Bahar screamed. "You're going to die now."

The helicopter began to pitch and yaw, sending Hawk in search of something to maintain his balance. He grabbed onto the back of the co-pilot's seat in an effort to keep from falling out of the aircraft.

Out of the corner of Hawk's eye, he noticed the pilot brandishing a gun. Hawk glanced outside and saw they were still close to the water, near enough for him to survive a leap. Once he figured it was safe enough, he didn't hesitate and dove out of the chopper.

He hit the water hard but maintained his consciousness. After regaining his bearings, he started treading water. He looked up to see the helicopter circling around him. Lit by the chopper's external lights, Bahar was kneeling down, clutching a bar near the doorway as she stared at him. He half expected her to shoot, but she didn't, instead gesturing and saying something before the helicopter peeled off and turned north.

Hawk took a deep breath and began his long swim to shore.

CHAPTER 30

HAWK STAGGERED OUT of the water and then collapsed onto the beach. Every muscle in his body was aching from the swim that he estimated to be at least two miles. His workout regimen often included swimming, but never two miles. He was certain he could feel muscles he never even knew existed.

The water rushed over him in both directions as high tide had come and gone. The pale moon overhead provided just enough light for Hawk to tell where he was—and that he was alone. He wanted to get up, but he couldn't convince his body to comply. Exhausted, he decided to close his eyes for just a moment so he could regain his strength.

He didn't know how long he'd been out when he felt a solid object hit him hard in the back. Hawk spun around to look up and see who had caught him, hoping he wasn't about to see Evana Bahar's face.

"So, the legends aren't true—Brady Hawk is

human after all," a woman said.

Hawk blinked several times, his eyes attempting to adjust to the dim light. But he recognized the voice first.

"Alex," he said. "Can you help me to my feet?"

"Sure, cowboy. If you wanted to take a nap on the beach this badly, you didn't have to jump out of a helicopter to do it."

"Did you see what happened?" he asked.

She shook her head. "I watched the helicopter fluttering over the bay like something was wrong. And then I saw you hanging from the skids like a moron. But then I had my own problems."

"I guess they aren't your problems any more since I don't see any flashing lights in the distance."

"Yeah, they're gone for now, but for how long is the question I don't want to know the answer to. Let's get the hell outta here."

"Roger that," Hawk said.

Alex opened the door for him and helped him inside. She eased into the driver's side seat and turned the key, igniting the engine. It purred as Hawk pulled the harness across his chest.

"Please, no more chases," Hawk said. "I've had enough erratic driving and piloting for one day."

"I won't make any promises," Alex said with a wink.

Hawk looked at the clock—it was nearly 1:00 a.m. While Hawk's body had reached its limit, his mind was still working.

"Do you still have those missiles in the trunk?" he asked.

Alex nodded. "What are you thinking?"

"We need to get rid of those things right now."

"And how do you propose to do that?"

"Let's sink them in the bay."

Alex pulled into an empty beach parking lot just off the main road.

"Remove all the navigational features," Hawk said. "Basically take out anything that could be used to reverse engineer these weapons."

"I'm already on it," Alex said, unscrewing the control panel that contained the navigational device for each missile.

Less than ten minutes later, she had stripped each missile down to little more than its shell.

"They're awfully light," Alex said as she weighed one in her hands. "Are you sure these things will sink?"

Hawk nodded. "Even if they don't, it won't matter. The Cubans—or anyone else for that matter—won't be able to do anything with them."

Satisfied that the missiles were unusable and the chemicals would be rendered useless, he headed toward the mainland. Once they started to cross the bridge that spanned an inlet, Alex eased onto the shoulder. She tossed the first missile into the water. The moon provided just enough light for her to see the weapon disappear beneath the surface. She proceeded to dispose of the other two, lingering until they vanished in the water.

Hawk watched from the comfort of the car.

"Good work, Alex," he said after she returned.

"Let's get out of here."

Hawk dialed Blunt's number.

"You both still alive?" Blunt asked.

"For the time being," Hawk said. "But just barely."

"I look forward to hearing all about it. Apparently you succeeded."

"We tried calling you earlier, but you didn't answer your phone, which isn't like you. Is everything okay?"

"It is now. I'll fill you in on everything when you get back."

"Yeah, about that," Hawk said. "We need to get out of here ASAP. Can you contact the pilot for us and have him report to the airport immediately?"

"What did you do?"

"Don't worry. We didn't leave a trail of dead bodies, but we could be in some hot water if we're still here in the morning."

"I'll call the pilot and have him get the plane ready."

Hawk hung up and looked at Alex. "We're getting out of here tonight."

* * *

AN HOUR LATER, Hawk and Alex were taxiing down the runway.

"I'm not gonna miss this place," Alex said.

"If only we had a chance to spend some time relaxing at the beach," Hawk said.

"I think I'm starting to see the allure of a beach vacation."

"I knew you'd come around."

The plane sped down the runway before lifting off.

As the aircraft climbed, Alex looked at her phone and noticed she'd missed a call from Mallory along with a couple of texts.

Alex scrolled through the pictures that Mallory had sent, including the image painted on her wall. After studying them, Alex handed her phone to Hawk.

"Chilling," he said once he'd finished and returned her cell. "I wonder what she's stumbled on."

"Well, she mentioned about seeing an image of a pair of senators meeting with some Chinese Navy admirals in a meeting that wasn't made public."

"Of course they wouldn't want that getting out,

but maybe it's not what it seems."

She forced a laugh. "When is any clandestine meeting with politicians benign? There's a reason they don't want that information getting out."

"Whatever the reason, it looks like she's poked the bear. We need to speak with Blunt about this when we get back and see if he knows anything."

Alex nodded. "That's not all Mallory sent me. There's also this dossier that I thought you might find interesting."

She handed the phone back to him. He scanned a report, complete with pictures. Hawk zoomed in on the images and shook his head.

"This isn't exactly news to me now," Hawk said after he read the document.

"I know, but I thought you'd want to see that intelligence briefing. Evana Bahar has breathed new life into Al Hasib, only she's renamed it *Al Fatihin*—The Conquerors."

Hawk sighed. "I guess we can forget about beach vacations any time soon."

CHAPTER 31

Langley, Virginia

GENERAL FORTNER HUNG UP after getting debriefed by Blunt. Digesting the news wasn't easy for Fortner, who was tasked with gathering intelligence to keep U.S. interests safe. The notion that someone would conspire against his own country to move an agenda forward wasn't unique, but the fact that it was Senator Thurman shocked Fortner. Thurman's presidential aspirations were no secret, even something people within the intelligence community rooted for despite being urged to remain neutral politically. However, working in cooperation with a terrorist organization to assassinate the sitting president wasn't an act that could be ignored.

Fortner paced around the room, considering the best way to break the news to President Young. A face-to-face meeting would be best, but Young wasn't likely to peel off his stumping schedule at a time when his party needed him to bolster their chances in the mid-term elections. And while Fortner contemplated meeting Young on the campaign trail, reports of such a meeting could get leaked to the press and lead to wild speculation. Ultimately, Fortner decided a phone call was his best option.

Fortner alerted Young's staff about an urgent conversation that needed to occur. Fifteen minutes later, Fortner's phone rang.

"Please stay on the line for the President of the United States," a woman said.

After several clicks, Young started speaking. "General, how the hell are ya?"

"I'm doing well, but I wish I had better news for you."

"What's going on?"

"Actually, it's already happened and everyone is safe, but I thought you might be interested to know that an attempt was made on your life at the Hard Rock Stadium last night."

"What?" Young asked with an edge to his voice. "And this is the first I'm hearing of it?"

"I just found out about it myself."

"Why didn't my Secret Service detail know? Were they in on it?"

"No, no. Nothing like that. No one knew about it because the attack was launched from offshore."

"A missile attack?"

"*Chemical* weapons, sir. But a pair of agents from The Phoenix Foundation was able to stop the attack from its origin in Cuba. They were able to divert the missile and guide it safely into the Atlantic."

"Who was responsible for this?"

"The terrorist organization Al Fatihin, which is basically the resurrected version of Al Hasib."

"Dammit. I thought we eliminated them."

"Well, they weren't the only ones associated with the attack."

"Who else was involved?"

"Al Fatihin was aided and abetted by one of our own senators, Lon Thurman."

"Thurman? Are you sure? We've been friends for a long time."

"We have proof that he's the one who was behind all this. However, the way we gathered some of the evidence against him might not be considered admissible in a court of law. Plus, I'm not sure what you think about how such a high-profile court case would play among the public."

"It'd just further divide the country, if that's even possible," Young said.

"Thurman knows we're on to him, but I think he believes he's untouchable due to his relationship with you."

"If he's trying to kill me, that kind of changes things."

Fortner sighed. "Perhaps he thinks he can convince you that it's a conspiracy against him, that the Russians are trying to frame him for murdering his son."

"Did they kill Thaxton?"

"Technically, yes. But we believe Thurman engaged a Russian assassin to carry out the deed."

"But why would he kill his own son?

"Thaxton discovered what his father was up to and confronted him about it. Apparently, the senator didn't care for that. The bigger question I have is why he would want to assassinate you."

Young took a deep breath before continuing. "Ever since Thurman entered politics, people around him have been grooming him to become President one day. He had a strong resume, but he felt like he was lacking one more thing—a cabinet post."

"And you didn't offer him one?"

"Initially we talked about him serving as the Secretary of State, but I later decided to go in another direction. I knew he was upset about it, but I didn't imagine he'd try to kill me. What could he possibly stand to gain from that?"

"He has a close relationship with your vice president," Fortner said. "Perhaps he thought with you out of the picture that he could get what he wanted through a different route."

"This is infuriating and disappointing," Young said.

"The only question now is how do you want us to handle it? We could pass all this information along to the FBI and see if they'd want to take a crack at prosecuting him for all these crimes."

"No, let's handle this quietly. I think you know what needs to be done."

"You've got it, sir."

CHAPTER 32

BLUNT TOOK A LONG PULL from his glass and then swirled the amber liquid around before draining it. It was the first day in a week that the weather had cooled off enough for him to sit outside on his porch in the evening, something he didn't imagine possible when temperatures were soaring near 100 degrees Fahrenheit. But much can change in one week.

It was only a week ago that he was musing how content he was to ride out the rest of his working days, squashing terrorists from his cushy third-floor office at The Phoenix Foundation. He glanced down at the flash drive on his coffee table. Everything changed when he saw the contents on the device. Names, organizations, affiliations, methods to control various elements of economy and government. All of it was deeply disconcerting.

His phone buzzed with a text from Hawk. He and Alex were at the door.

Blunt lumbered through the house and opened the door, allowing his guests inside without much in the way of a greeting. A half-hearted wave ushered them into his house.

"I'm out back," Blunt said, already heading toward the porch.

"And drinking," Alex said.

"Come join me," he said. "We have plenty of reasons to drink."

Hawk and Alex settled into wicker chairs across from Blunt.

"I assume you heard the news about Senator Thurman," Hawk said.

Blunt shook his head. "I've had too many things on my mind. What happened?"

"Died of a heart attack last night."

Blunt grunted. "Serves the bastard right. Anybody who has his own son murdered doesn't deserve to live anyway."

Alex got up and grabbed a pair of tumblers from the wet bar. She poured a pair of drinks for herself and Hawk before returning to her seat.

"So what's got you in this mood?" Alex asked.

"Do you remember Lee Hendridge?"

"Yeah, how could I forget?" Alex asked. "The tenacious journalist who was murdered after helping us out."

"Well, I met his former girlfriend, Rebecca Paris. She came to me about a week ago and told me that Lee wasn't murdered for helping us. He was killed because of something else he was looking into. Long story short, it turns out he uncovered the existence of a group called Obsidian, which is a network of powerful people from various countries to control everything from food prices and production, to oil to banking and to government policies. It's basically a shadow government ruling everything. Lee was going to expose all those involved."

"Sounds depressing," Hawk said.

"It is, but mostly because I just wanted The Phoenix Foundation to focus on working with the CIA on special projects. You know, the easy stuff. But this is a real threat to freedom everywhere and demands our attention."

"I wonder if that's what Mallory stumbled onto," Alex said.

"What happened to her?"

"She found some images at the NSA of two senators meeting with four Chinese Navy admirals. After she mentioned it to me, someone broke into her house and ransacked it. They left this symbol on the wall, but she couldn't find it anywhere on the internet or in the NSA archives."

Alex held up her phone for Blunt to see. He studied the picture for a moment and then nodded.

"Lee had a couple pictures with that symbol in them. That's the work of Obsidian all right."

"So, what are we gonna do about it?" Alex asked.

"We have to approach this carefully. That means no texts, no emails, and no phone calls. All of our correspondence and communication regarding this group has to be done old school. Handwritten notes that we destroy after viewing. And after today, private conversations in locations where no one can hear us. It's too risky to operate any other way. But we're going to have to juggle this operation along with all our regular assignments so we won't be drawing any suspicion from Obsidian. For all we know, this list could just be a partial one, and even outdated at that. We can't let anyone—not even Fortner—know about what we're up to. If word of this leaks, it could spell disaster for all of us."

"What about the information we retrieved from Venice? Are we just going to put that on the backburner?" Alex asked.

"Funny that you should ask that," Blunt said. "Guess whose name was on Lee Hendridge's list?"

Alex shrugged.

"Andrei Orlovsky, the Russian arms dealer," Blunt said.

"Meaning that his contacts could also be working

with Obsidian?"

"That's what I'm thinking, but we'll have to sort all that out."

"Sounds like loads of fun," Hawk said, clapping his hands and rubbing them together. "Where do we start?"

"It's interesting that you bring up the Chinese admirals, because we're going after one first," Blunt said. "However, he's not an admiral for the Chinese—he's one of our own. Our first target from Lee's spreadsheet will be Admiral Bart Adelman."

Hawk froze. "What name did you say?"

"Admiral Bart Adelamn. You know him?"

Hawk nodded. "He was my first commander when I was in the Navy SEALS."

"You just never know about people, do you?" Blunt asked.

Hawk shook his head. "No, you don't."

Blunt set his glass down and stood. "Well, that's enough of sitting around feeling sorry for ourselves. It's time to get to work."

THE END

ACKNOWLEDGMENTS

I am grateful to so many people who have helped with the creation of this project and the entire Brady Hawk series.

Krystal Wade was a big help in editing this book as always.

I would also like to thank my advance reader team for all their input in improving this book along with all the other readers who have enthusiastically embraced the story of Brady Hawk. Stay tuned ... there's more Brady Hawk coming soon.

ABOUT THE AUTHOR

R.J. PATTERSON is an award-winning writer living in southeastern Idaho. He first began his illustrious writing career as a sports journalist, recording his exploits on the soccer fields in England as a young boy. Then when his father told him that people would pay him to watch sports if he would write about what he saw, he went all in. He landed his first writing job at age 15 as a sports writer for a daily newspaper in Orangeburg, S.C. He later attended earned a degree in newspaper journalism from the University of Georgia, where he took a job covering high school sports for the award-winning *Athens Banner-Herald* and *Daily News*.

He later became the sports editor of *The Valdosta Daily Times* before working in the magazine world as an editor and freelance journalist. He has won numerous writing awards, including a national award for his investigative reporting on a sordid tale surrounding an NCAA investigation over the University of Georgia football program.

R.J. enjoys the great outdoors of the Northwest while living there with his wife and four children. He still follows sports closely. He also loves connecting with readers and would love to hear from you. To stay updated about future projects, connect with him over Facebook or on the inter-webs at www.RJPbooks.com and sign up for his newsletter to get deals and updates.

Made in the USA
Monee, IL
30 June 2022

98863047R00163